A Word from Stephanie
about the Ups and Downs
of Friendship

I'm not usually a suspicious person. But when a Flamingo tries to be nice, I say, be careful! Members of that creepy club just can't be trusted. Especially because we were about to pitch all-out war against the Flamingoes—on the ski slopes. It was our biggest school trip of the year, and Darcy, Allie, and I were a solid team in every sense of the word. We planned to eat together, bunk together, ski together, and win the big race together. So when Melody Kimball tried to worm her way into our threesome, I figured it was some kind of trick. And, suddenly, someone started finding out all our team secrets. Hmmm. Whom would you suspect? But before I tell you who the secret spy turned out to be, let me tell you about another type of team—my family, and our crazy household.

Right now there are nine people and a dog living in our house—and for all I know, someone new could move in at any time. There's me, my big sister, D.J., my little sister, Michelle, and my dad, Danny. But that's just the beginning.

When my mom died, Dad needed help. So he asked his old college buddy, Joey Gladstone, and my

Uncle Jesse to come live with us, to help take care of me and my sisters.

Back then, Uncle Jesse didn't know much about taking care of three little girls. He was more into rock 'n' roll. Joey didn't know anything about kids, either—but it sure was funny watching him learn!

Having Uncle Jesse and Joey around was like having three dads instead of one! But then something even better happened—Uncle Jesse fell in love. He married Rebecca Donaldson, Dad's co-host on his TV show, *Wake Up, San Francisco*. Aunt Becky's so nice—she's more like a big sister than an aunt.

Next Uncle Jesse and Aunt Becky had twin baby boys. Their names are Nicky and Alex, and they are adorable!

I love being part of a big family. Still, things can get pretty crazy when you live in such a full house!

FULL HOUSE™: Stephanie novels

Phone Call from a Flamingo
The Boy-Oh-Boy Next Door
Twin Troubles
Hip Hop Till You Drop
Here Comes the Brand-New Me
The Secret's Out
Daddy's Not-So-Little Girl
P.S. Friends Forever
Getting Even with the Flamingoes
The Dude of My Dreams
Back-to-School Cool
Picture Me Famous
Two-for-One Christmas Fun
The Big Fix-up Mix-up
Ten Ways to Wreck a Date
Wish Upon a VCR
Doubles or Nothing
Sugar and Spice Advice
Never Trust a Flamingo

Available from MINSTREL Books

FULL HOUSE™
Stephanie

Never Trust a Flamingo

Devra Newberger Speregen

A Parachute Press Book

FAMILY ENTERTAINMENT
READING

A
MINSTREL®
BOOK

Published by POCKET BOOKS
New York   London   Toronto   Sydney   Tokyo   Singapore

A MINSTREL PAPERBACK *Original*

 A Minstrel Book published by
POCKET BOOKS, a division of Simon & Schuster Inc.
1230 Avenue of the Americas, New York, NY 10020

A PARACHUTE PRESS BOOK

 READING Copyright © and ™ 1996 by Warner Bros.

FULL HOUSE, characters, names and all related indicia are trademarks of Warner Bros. © 1996.

ISBN: 0-671-56843-4

First Minstrel Books printing December 1996

10 9 8 7 6 5 4 3 2 1

A MINSTREL BOOK and colophon are registered trademarks of Simon & Schuster Inc.

Cover photo by Schultz Photography

Printed in the U.S.A.

CHAPTER
1

◆ ◀ ◗ ◆

"Where *are* those dumb house keys, anyway?"

Stephanie Tanner pushed her long blond hair out of her eyes. "I'm sure I put them in my backpack this morning!"

Stephanie sat down on on the curb. She peered inside her backpack. "Found them!" she exclaimed with a sigh of relief.

She dug out her keys from the bottom of her backpack, where they were hidden under her hairbrush.

Her best friend, Allie Taylor, sat down beside her. "Stephanie! Did you hear anything I just said?" Allie asked.

Allie's brow was wrinkled and her lips were pursed together. Stephanie had seen that look hundreds of times. It was the face Allie made when she was annoyed. She'd made the same face back in kindergarten, where she and Stephanie had first met.

Allie had wavy, light brown hair and light green eyes. She could be quiet and shy, but she and Stephanie had lots in common. They both loved music, reading, and funny movies.

"Sorry, Al," Stephanie told her. "I didn't hear. What were you asking?"

Allie sighed. "For the *third* time, I asked you if you had a ski jacket to wear for the school ski trip."

"No," Stephanie said. "But D.J. has one. I'm hoping she'll lend it to me." D.J. was Stephanie's older sister. She was eighteen and took classes at a nearby college.

"Isn't D.J. pretty touchy about sharing clothes?" Allie asked.

"Yeah," Stephanie answered. "But I figured she won't care much about the ski jacket. I can't remember the last time she even wore the thing."

Darcy Powell, Stephanie's other best friend, sat down on the curb next to Stephanie and Allie. Darcy had brown hair and deep brown eyes. She had tons of energy and a great sense of humor. Darcy had been best friends with Stephanie and Allie since sixth grade.

"Is it down?" Darcy asked Stephanie.

Stephanie glanced at Darcy and then at the ground. "Is what down?" she asked in confusion.

"The jacket," Darcy explained. "Is it stuffed with down feathers? It's the best kind of jacket when you ski. Down is the warmest."

Stephanie shrugged. "I don't know," she said.

"Well, if it isn't down," Darcy went on, "you can borrow my old parka."

"Thanks, Darce!" Stephanie said.

"No problem," Darcy said.

Stephanie got up and slung her backpack over her shoulder. Darcy and Allie stood also. They headed toward Stephanie's house. Stephanie stuffed one hand into her jacket pocket as she hurried up the driveway to the front door. She stopped short.

"What's this?" she muttered. She pulled a folded piece of paper from her pocket. She unfolded it and gasped in horror.

"My permission slip!" she cried.

"For the ski trip?" Allie asked in alarm. "You mean you didn't hand it in yet?"

"It's supposed to be in by tomorrow," Darcy pointed out.

Stephanie stared at the form. "I forgot all about it," she admitted. Her stomach twisted.

"Well, it's signed, at least. Isn't it?" Darcy asked.

"Not exactly," Stephanie said.

"Stephanie, get your dad to sign it *tonight!*" Allie exclaimed. "The trip is this Saturday!"

"And it's going to be the most excellent trip of the year," Darcy added.

"I know, I know," Stephanie replied. "But getting this signed won't be so easy."

Darcy scrunched up her nose. "What do you mean?"

"I mean this." Stephanie read part of the form out loud: *"The Firewood Ski Lodge will not be held responsible for any slips, falls, or accidents that occur as a result of insufficient ski training. Skiers ski at their own risk."*

"So?" Darcy asked.

"So my dad will flip out when he reads this," Stephanie explained. "You know what a worrier he is. He hates anything that might be even a little dangerous. He even makes Michelle wear knee pads when she plays hopscotch!"

"But doesn't anyone in your family ski?" Allie asked.

"Yeah, I mean, if someone else skiied, maybe they could convince your dad that it's a safe sport," Darcy said.

"Sure," Allie agreed. "Someone in your house *must* be a skiier!"

Stephanie had a pretty big family. Nine people lived in her house. Besides Stephanie and her dad and D.J. there was Michelle, Stephanie's nine-year-old sister. Then there were her uncle Jesse and his wife, Becky. Jesse and Becky had four-year-old twins, Alex and Nicky. They all shared an apartment in the attic.

The other member of the family was Joey Gladstone. Joey was her dad's best friend from college. He had lived with the family since Stephanie was very small.

"Joey went skiing once or twice," Stephanie said.

"Great! Then he can tell your dad how safe it is," Darcy replied.

"No way," Stephanie insisted. "The last time Joey went skiing, he sprained his arm."

"Ouch! I guess he fell on a really steep slope or something, right?" Darcy asked.

"No, he wasn't even skiing!" Stephanie answered. "He slipped on some ice in the parking lot. But Dad didn't care. He said skiing was too dangerous for anyone. He swore that he'd never let any of us go skiing. Ever."

"Still, there's got to be some way we can convince him to let you go," Allie said.

Darcy nodded. "Sure. After all, skiing is very good exercise. And it's good for the heart. And the lungs."

"Darcy's right," Allie agreed. "Plus you're a pretty good athlete, Steph. If you're careful, you shouldn't get hurt at all."

Stephanie shrugged. "Maybe."

"Definitely," Allie said. "Don't forget, Darcy's gone skiing with her family lots of times." she turned to her friend. "Darcy, you can teach Stephanie how to ski safely, can't you?"

Darcy nodded to Stephanie. "No problem. And maybe my dad can call your dad and tell him there's nothing to worry about."

"That would be great!" Stephanie exclaimed. "Because I really, really want to go on this trip!"

"What trip?" Michelle asked. She had just come home from school. "What are you guys doing standing around out here?" Michelle added.

Stephanie groaned. "What do you care, Michelle? It's bad enough sharing a bedroom with you," she said. "Do you *always* have to know every little detail of my life?"

"Never mind," Michelle answered. "I don't care anyway." Michelle hurried to the front door. She took out her own keys and let herself inside.

Stephanie, Darcy, and Allie followed her. Michelle headed into the kitchen, so Stephanie and her friends settled on the living room couch.

"Maybe we could rent one of those how to tapes about skiing before the trip," Allie suggested.

Stephanie nodded. "Not a bad idea." She turned to Darcy. "Pass me a pen and some paper, Darce. I'll write all these ideas down." She began a list of their suggestions.

"I could go to the library tonight and get some skiing books," Darcy added.

"Great. My dad's big on going to the library to look up stuff," Stephanie told her.

"And I can loan you my knee pads," Darcy offered. "And my bike helmet, if you want." She and Allie chuckled.

"Very funny," Stephanie said.

"No, really," Darcy said. "You don't have to actually *wear* them. Just make sure your father sees you *pack* them. Then keep them in your duffel bag during the trip."

Stephanie tapped the end of the pen on her chin. "Actually that *isn't* a bad idea. I could make a big production about packing all that safety equipment."

She added that idea to her list.

7

Michelle hurried into the living room, carrying a cupcake and a glass of milk. "What are you guys talking about?" she asked.

"Nothing," Stephanie replied. "Uh, Michelle, can we have a little privacy here?"

Michelle made a face. "It's my living room, too!" she protested.

Stephanie rolled her eyes. It was the same old argument with her sister, day after day. "Come on, Michelle! We're really busy!"

"So?" Michelle plopped down on the floor next to the coffee table to eat her snack.

Stephanie groaned loudly. "Fine, Michelle. Be a baby. Stay." Stephanie leaned toward her friends. "Just ignore her," she said loudly. "Little sisters are such pests!"

"Never mind. I'm not staying," Michelle said. She picked up her food and headed back to the kitchen.

"Good!" Stephanie said when she was gone. "Michelle is driving me totally crazy. She never leaves me alone anymore."

"That's why it's totally important for you to come on this trip," Allie pointed out. "You need time away from Michelle."

"Do I ever!" Stephanie agreed.

"So you should learn a couple of very safe skiing moves," Darcy told her. "To show your dad."

Darcy leaped off the sofa. She hurried onto the landing by the front door. "Come here, Steph. I'll show you how to do the most important safety move there is."

"What's that?" Stephanie asked. "Turning? Or jumping?"

Darcy grinned. "No . . . *stopping!*"

Allie and Stephanie exchanged looks of surprise. "Stopping?" Stephanie said. "It doesn't sound very exciting."

"No, but it's really an important thing to learn. Now do what I do." Darcy stood with her legs together and bent her knees. Stephanie stood next to her and copied Darcy's movements.

"Good, Stephanie! Now bring your toes together and dig your heels into the snow, er . . . the carpet. That's perfect. You got it right on the first try!" Darcy exclaimed.

Allie laughed. "Stephanie, you look completely ridiculous!"

Stephanie grinned and flapped her arms like wings. "Check this out! It's the Funky Chicken on skis!" she cried.

Allie and Darcy cracked up.

"Come on, Stephanie!" Darcy said in between giggles. "Get serious!"

Stephanie spied two umbrellas next to the front door. "I am serious," she joked. She grabbed the umbrellas and tucked them under her arms as if they were ski poles.

"It's Hotdoggin' Tanner!" she cried. "The world's fastest downhill racer!" She crouched down and swayed from side to side.

"Swoosh! Hotdoggin' Tanner is hot today, folks! She leans to the left! She leans to the right! She soars through the toughest ski course known to mankind! And now, for her big finale . . . a double-triple flip—in midair!"

Stephanie tossed aside the umbrellas and jumped high into the air.

At that moment the front door swung open. Danny Tanner, Stephanie's dad, stepped briskly inside.

"Yahooooo!" Stephanie shouted. She landed on the carpet and turned two somersaults. "And there's not a scratch on her!" she yelled.

"Why would there be any scratches on you?" her father demanded.

Gulp!

"Uh, hi, Dad!" Stephanie said. "I didn't see you there."

"Stephanie, why are you jumping around the living room?" Danny frowned.

Stephanie bit her bottom lip. "Um, I was just . . . uh . . ." She glanced nervously at her friends.

"Go ahead," Darcy whispered.

"Tell him," Allie urged.

"Tell me what?" her father demanded.

CHAPTER
2

♦ ◀ ◗ ♦

"Uh, tell you what I was practicing," Stephanie said.

Danny hung his coat neatly on the clothes rack by the front door. "This isn't a gym, you know," Danny said. "What could you be practicing here? Breaking your legs?" He laughed out loud.

Stephanie laughed loudly along. "Breaking my legs? Ha! That's funny, Dad! That's a good one!"

Danny eyed Stephanie suspiciously. "It wasn't *that* good, Stephanie," he said.

"True," Stephanie answered. "Um, the truth is, I have to show you something."

She hurried to the coffee table and found the permission slip. She smoothed it out and thrust it toward her father.

"What's this?" Danny asked.

"A permission slip for an overnight school trip," Stephanie answered. "The trip is this weekend. Can I go?"

Danny smiled. "An overnight trip? That sounds like fun! Where are you going? To Napa Valley? The Hearst Castle?"

Stephanie handed her father a pen. "Sign right here," she said. She pointed to the blank space next to the words *Signature of Parent or Guardian*.

She tried to cover the rest of the slip with her hand.

Danny chuckled. "Hold on, honey. I want to read this entire form first," he said.

Stephanie sighed and moved her hand away.

Her father read every word of the permission slip. Stephanie watched his face. She winced as he stopped smiling.

"Skiing?" he blurted. "No way, Stephanie. You know how I feel about skiing. It's very dangerous!"

"But Dad! The whole school is going!" Stephanie protested. "And I'll be careful, I promise!"

"It's not that I think you'll be careless," Danny said. "It's just that skiing is a very dangerous sport."

"Um, Mr. Tanner," Darcy began. "My father goes skiing with us all the time. You can call him and ask him how safe skiing can be. He'd be glad to talk to you."

Danny smiled. "That's very nice of you, Darcy. But my mind is made up. This is one trip that Stephanie will have to miss."

Stephanie was on the verge of panic. This was terrible! She needed to think of something. And *fast*.

"Wait, Dad. Would you talk to Mr. Merin?" she asked. "He's the teacher who's in charge of the trip."

Danny thought it over. "Mr. Merin?" he said. "I have always liked Mr. Merin." Danny had met Stephanie's media studies teacher earlier that year at a parent-teacher conference.

Danny Tanner was the cohost of a local TV show, *Good Morning, San Francisco*. Mr. Merin knew a lot about television production. They had discussed television together for the whole conference.

Danny nodded. "Okay," he finally said. "I'll call him tomorrow. That's a promise."

Danny left the room. Darcy and Allie got ready to go. Stephanie walked them to the front door.

"Thanks anyway, you guys," she said. "You tried."

"If there's anything else we can do, just call," Darcy said.

Stephanie nodded, then closed the door behind them. This was by far the worst day of her life.

She couldn't believe that she might actually miss the most excellent school trip of the whole year!

CHAPTER
3

◆ ◢ ◗ ◆

"Stephanie!" Darcy shouted across the lunchroom. "Did you hear about the trip yet?"

Darcy hurried over to their lunch table.

Stephanie shook her head. "No, not yet."

"Stephanie! Wait!" Another shout rang out.

Allie raced to the table. "What happened?" she asked.

"Relax, Allie. Stephanie's dad didn't talk to Mr. Merin yet," Darcy told her. "We're still waiting."

"Oh." Allie sighed and sat down with her friends.

"Well, don't worry, Stephanie," Allie said. "I think Mr. Merin will convince your dad to let you go on the trip. I have a good feeling about this."

"Oh, you know what I forgot to tell you?" Stephanie asked. "I heard Kyle Sullivan is going on the trip. He—"

"Kyle Sullivan!" Allie exclaimed. "Are you joking?

She and Darcy exchanged knowing looks.

"I thought you were finished with your crush on Kyle!" Darcy exclaimed.

"I am! I am!" Stephanie insisted. "We had that one date, and it was pretty awful. But we're still friends," she added.

Allie and Darcy seemed relieved. Stephanie knew they didn't want to hear her talk about Kyle Sullivan. For months she had driven them crazy, talking about Kyle.

"My monster crush is history," Stephanie assured them. "One date with Kyle proved that. I mean, he was the bossiest, most impossible date ever."

"Well, I almost forgot something, too," Allie said. "Do you know who *I* heard is going on the trip?"

"Tell us," Stephanie said. "Who?"

"Rene Salter," Allie announced.

"Rene? Ugh!" Stephanie said. She made a gagging noise.

Rene was in ninth grade. She was the leader of the Flamingoes. The Flamingoes were a group of girls at Stephanie's school who thought they were the best-looking, most popular girls around. Stephanie and her friends thought they were the most obnoxious—and the most snobby.

Stephanie and Allie had been asked to join the club. That was two years ago. The Flamingoes had made them do terrible things. They made them lie to their friends. They even tricked Stephanie into stealing her father's phone card.

Luckily Stephanie had figured out what was happening. She and Allie both quit the club. The Flamingoes had it in for them ever since. Then this year things got even worse.

Everyone at school knew that Rene really liked Kyle Sullivan. But Kyle had asked Stephanie on a date first. Rene was jealous. Now she was even ruder and nastier than before.

"What about the other Flamingoes?" Stephanie asked. "Are they going on the skiing trip, too?"

"Most of them," Allie replied. "Mary, Julie, Alyssa, and that other girl, Melody."

Mary Kelly was Rene's best friend. Stephanie thought Mary was just almost as rude and obnoxious as Rene. Plus Mary was a huge snob. She made fun of kids right to their faces. Julie Chu wasn't as mean, but she had a really superior attitude. She was always chewing gum and acting totally bored by everything and anyone who wasn't a Flamingo.

Stephanie didn't know Julie or Mary very well. Alyssa Norman usually kept pretty quiet. She just followed Rene around and did whatever Rene said. And Melody Kimball was new to the school, so Stephanie didn't know her at all. But she assumed Alyssa and Melody were just as obnoxious as Rene and the others.

"So much for our fun weekend," Stephanie muttered. "Those Flamingoes will ruin this trip."

Allie stared at her two friends. "Come on, you guys! Just because the Flamingoes are going doesn't mean we can't have fun! We'll just pretend they're not there. We'll avoid them totally!"

Stephanie thought for a moment. "You know, you're right. We should ignore her. In fact, we could ignore *all* the Flamingoes! After all, it's only a two-day trip."

Allie grinned. "That's the spirit! Think positive!"

"You mean think snow!" Stephanie giggled.

"And that reminds me of something else," Darcy said. She reached under the table and lifted her shopping bag. She dug into it and pulled out and enormous, bright orange ski parka.

"Check this out, Stephanie!" she exclaimed excitedly. "It's the down jacket I was telling you about. Isn't it awesome?"

Stephanie's mouth hung open. "Uh . . . it's . . . it's very *orange*," she managed to say.

"And it looks enormous," Allie added.

Darcy frowned. "It's oversize," she said. "Well, not really. Actually it used to be my mom's. She's bigger than me. And then it was my older sister's, and then it was mine. But I got a new one for Christmas, so you can borrow this one if you want."

"I don't know." Stephanie hesitated. Sure, the jacket looked warm enough, but it was so . . . so . . . *orange*.

"Come on! Try it on!" Darcy said.

"Okay, I'll try it." Stephanie pulled on the jacket.

It *was* big—Stephanie's hands barely stuck out from the sleeves. But it was also really comfortable.

A familiar—and very annoying—voice suddenly rang out behind her. "Look, guys! It's the Great Pumpkin!"

Stephanie whirled around. And found herself face to face with Rene. Rene was wearing a ski jacket, too. And so were the Flamingoes standing with her—Mary, Alyssa, Julie, and Melody. All their jackets were the exact same color: bright pink, with their names stitched in darker pink on the front.

"Well, you won't have to worry about getting lost on this trip," Rene added with a smirk. "You'll be easy to spot. Just look for the fat orange beach ball rolling down the mountain!"

Mary and Julie cracked up. Some kids sitting at a nearby table laughed also. Stephanie blushed in embarrassment.

"Hey," Rene went on, "we Flamingoes better stick close to Stephanie on the slopes. If we get lost in a blizzard or something, we can use her jacket to call for help—instead of flares!"

Mary and Julie laughed harder than ever. Alyssa snorted.

"Well, at least she won't be mistaken for a wad of chewed-up bubble gum," Melody Kimball blurted.

"What?" Rene stared at Melody. So did Stephanie. And Darcy and Allie. Melody grinned. Her brown eyes twinkled. She pushed back her reddish brown bangs from her forehead.

"Come on, Rene," Melody went on. "Admit it. This color pink is about as about as attractive as a bottle of Pepto-Bismol. You know, upset-stomach medicine."

Stephanie's mouth fell open. She gaped at Melody in astonishment. The other Flamingoes seemed confused.

Rene ignored her. "Anyway, Stephanie, I guess that parka—or whatever it is you're wearing—means you're going on the ski trip. I hope the mountain has a really big beginners slope. Or maybe I should call it the geek slope!"

Julie, Mary, and Alyssa laughed out loud. Rene smiled in triumph.

"Come on, you guys," Rene told them. "I've had enough of these losers. Let's get out of here."

When they were gone, Stephanie stared at her friends in amazement. "Did you guys hear what I heard? Melody just totally put down Rene! How cool was that?" She chuckled.

"What do you think Rene will do to Melody for saying that stuff? Make Melody carry her skis up the mountain? Or—I know! Rene will make Melody carry *Rene* up the mountain!" Stephanie bent over, she was laughing so hard.

Darcy giggled.

"Come on, Stephanie," Allie said impatiently. "We have more important things to do then talk about Flamingoes."

"Yeah, like finding out if your dad called Mr. Merin," Darcy added. "Let's go check."

Stephanie slipped off the orange parka. She

folded it neatly and slid it back into the shopping bag.

"Okay, you guys are right. Rene didn't pay much attention to what Melody said anyway. Too bad. It would be great if someone put Rene in her place." Stephanie slung her backpack over her shoulder. She grabbed the shopping bag. "Let's find Mr. Merin."

Stephanie followed Darcy and Allie to the teachers' lounge. But she couldn't help thinking about Melody teasing Rene.

Chewed-up bubble gum? Stomach medicine? Stephanie chuckled quietly to herself.

For a Flamingo, Melody Kimball was pretty funny!

CHAPTER
4

◆ ◀ ▶ ◆

When will Dad ever get home from work? Stephanie wondered for about the millionth time.

She never had found Mr. Merin after lunch, so she still didn't know how his conversation with her father turned out.

All this waiting is driving me nuts! she thought.

The front door swung open. Michelle entered and hung up her jacket.

"Oh. It's you," Stephanie said.

Michelle strolled into the living room. "Who should it be?" she asked. "Are you waiting for someone special?"

"Do you always have to know everything? Little sisters are such a pain," Stephanie grumbled.

"I was just asking!" Michelle complained. "I can ask a question, you know. It's a free country."

Stephanie sighed. "Fine. If you must know, I'm waiting to see if Dad is going to let me go on my school ski trip."

"Dad's never going to let you go, Stephanie," Michelle said. "He thinks watching skiing on TV is dangerous." Michelle laughed.

"Don't remind me!" Stephanie groaned. "There's probably no way Mr. Merin can convince him. I'm doomed."

"Doomed about what?" Danny Tanner walked through the front door.

"Dad! You're home!" Stephanie cried. "I can't take the waiting anymore! What happened with Mr. Merin? What did you decide?"

Danny hung up his coat and placed his briefcase by the door.

"Happy snow trails! You're going skiing!" Her father beamed at her and opened his arms wide.

"Yahoo!" Stephanie screamed. She ran to give her father a big hug. "Thank you! Thank you! Thank you!" she cried. "I can't wait to tell Allie and Darcy!"

Stephanie grabbed the phone and dialed Allie's number. "Get Darcy on the line, quick!" she ordered. Allie had special three-way calling, so they could all talk at the same time.

A moment later Darcy answered the phone.

"Guess what?" Stephanie shouted. "I'm going skiing!"

Darcy and Allie both started screaming. Stephanie held the phone away from her ear. Her friends were shrieking so loudly, she couldn't talk.

"This is fantastic!" Allie screeched.

"It sure is! So I think you should both come over here—" Stephanie began.

"Uh, Steph, honey?" Danny interrupted. He held up two ski jackets. One was bright red, the other was a shiny black. "Which one do you like best?" he asked.

Stephanie studied the two jackets. "The red, I guess," she said. "But I already have a ski jacket, Dad."

Danny laughed. "Oh, no, this isn't for you, sweetheart. It's for me."

Stephanie's eyes widened. "Huh? When are *you* going skiing?"

"I'm going with you," Danny answered. "On your school ski trip. I'm going to be a chaperone. They needed three parents to come along, and Mr. Merin asked me. Isn't it great?"

Stephanie clutched the phone to her chest. She

tried to keep her voice steady. "You're . . . going on my ski trip?" she asked.

Danny nodded enthusiastically.

"I'll . . . I'll call you guys back later," Stephanie mumbled into the phone. She hung up and stared at her father.

"It was Mr. Merin's idea," Danny told her. "And a perfect solution! This way you can have fun, and I can make sure you stay out of harm's way!"

Stephanie gulped. "Uh, that's great, Dad, except that I was counting on spending time with my friends. Not my family."

"Well, I bet you'll feel differently when I tell you who else is coming." Danny grinned.

"Um, who else is coming, Dad?" Stephanie said out loud.

Danny beamed at her. "Michelle! Won't that be fun? The three of us, learning how to ski together!"

CHAPTER
5

◆ ◀ ◆ ◆

Tweeeeeet! Tweeeeeet! Tweeeeeeeet!

Stephanie cringed. The high-pitched whistle felt as if it were blasting straight through her head. She buried her face against Allie's shoulder.

"Does he *have* to keep whistling at everyone?" She groaned.

Tweeeeeeeet!

"Okay, kids!" Danny shouted. "Let's form one single line on the curb! It's time to board the bus!"

It was five A.M. Saturday morning. Stephanie, Allie, and Darcy gathered in the parking lot of John Muir Middle School. Around them swarmed the other eighth and ninth graders who were going on the ski trip. There were about fifty kids in all. It was time to leave for the Tahoe Lodge and Ski

Resort. The resort was several hours away, and they needed to get an early start.

Stephanie pulled her jacket hood over her head and tied the drawstring. "Tell me when he gets on the bus," she whispered to her friends. "This is so embarrassing!"

Allie and Darcy laughed. "Oh, come on, Stephanie!" Darcy said. "He isn't that bad."

Stephanie peered through the hood. "Are you kidding? It's five o'clock in the morning, and my father is blowing a dopey whistle in front of the entire school."

Danny blew the whistle again. "Come on, campers!" he called.

Stephanie moaned. "Campers?" She winced. "This is going to be worse than I thought!"

She climbed the steps into the bus and headed toward the back—as far away from her father as possible. She plopped down in a seat behind Allie and Darcy. Seconds later Danny was standing over her.

"Steph, I have a favor to ask," he said. "Please watch after Michelle on the trip, okay? I have a lot of kids to keep track of and I need you to keep an eye on her."

Stephanie groaned. "But Dad," she whispered, "this is supposed to be *my* trip!"

Danny frowned. "But that doesn't mean you can ignore Michelle. Just sit with her on the bus ride."

"Dad, she's nine years old!" Stephanie protested. "How can I talk to my friends with her listening to every word I say?"

Danny shot her a stern look. "Stephanie, I don't have time to argue. Just do it!"

Danny hurried back to the front of the bus. Stephanie slumped down in her seat. Michelle skipped down the aisle and took the seat next to hers.

"Hey, Stephanie!" Michelle said. "Hi, Allie! Hi, Darcy! Look at my ski hat. I borrowed it from my friend Cassie." She waved the green pom-pom on the top of the hat at them.

"It's cute, Michelle," Allie said.

"Adorable," Stephanie grumbled.

Michelle smiled. "This is going to be so much fun!"

Stephanie stared out the window, muttering under her breath.

"It's just for the bus ride," Allie whispered to her. "When we get to the lodge, it'll be the three of us. Come on, cheer up! It'll be great!"

"It will?" Stephanie pointed at the front of the bus.

Rene and the other Flamingoes had just boarded

the bus. They were all wearing their pink ski jackets. Rene pointed at the back of the bus. "Let's grab seats to ourselves," she told the others in a loud voice.

A moment later the Flamingoes filed past Stephanie's seat. Rene suddenly stopped walking. She turned to her friends and said loudly, "Did you hear that annoying whistle? Who is that weird guy, anyway? The Mad Whistler?" The Flamingoes looked directly at Stephanie, then cracked up.

Stephanie pretended not to hear.

"That was our dad," Michelle said.

"Oh, really?" Rene turned to her friends and rolled her eyes. They cracked up again.

Melody sighed. "Let's just sit down already," she said.

"Sure," Rene said. "Let's take the last seats in the back. Then we can have a private club meeting."

The driver shut the bus door and started the engine. A loud cheer erupted as the bus pulled away from the school.

Mr. Merin stood up and turned on the bus microphone. "Hi, everyone!" he said. "Listen up! I'm going to read to you the ski trip schedule. But first I want you to meet our gracious parent chaperones. They've all volunteered to help us out on the trip.

31

This is Maria Cruz, Joan Spencer, and Danny Tanner."

At the mention of her father's name, Stephanie heard Rene's voice from the back of the bus. "Oh, the Mad Whistler is Stephanie's dad. It figures!" The Flamingoes all laughed. Stephanie sank even lower in her seat.

"We'll stop soon for breakfast," Mr. Merin continued. "Then we should arrive at the Tahoe Lodge at about nine A.M. After we unpack, we'll have the entire morning for skiing. Then at one o'clock it's time for lunch. After that more free ski time. Then at four we're having a sing-down."

"A sing-down! Cool!" Allie said.

"I love sing-downs," Michelle added. "We had them all the time at summer camp last year."

"Yeah, well, these are more grown-up sing-downs," Stephanie told her. "I'm sure they won't let you do it, anyway. I mean, these activities are for eighth and ninth graders."

"So?" Michelle folded her arms stubbornly across her chest. "Dad said I was allowed to do stuff with you."

"Now, listen, Michelle—" Stephanie started to say.

"Shhh! Hold on, Steph," Allie interrupted. "Mr. Merin isn't done talking."

"And then tonight will be very special," Mr. Merin was saying. "Dinner is at seven o'clock. Afterward we'll have a special scavenger hunt for everyone on the trip. Prizes will be awarded to the winners. Then there will be a big party in the lodge social hall."

There were more cheers and applause.

"Wait," Mr. Merin told them. "I've saved the best for last. Tomorrow morning you'll have plenty of skiing time. And then tomorrow afternoon we're having a relay race. Not just any race," he added. "A race on—snowboards!"

There were cheers and applause from the kids on the bus.

"Snowboards?" Stephanie said to Allie and Darcy. "Wow! That sounds way cool. But I've never snowboarded before."

"Anyone who wants to can sign up," Mr. Merin said. "I know most of you have never done any snowboarding. But we've scheduled a lesson for beginners before the race. That way the teams will be evenly matched."

Darcy turned around in her seat. "How cool is that?" she asked. "I tried snowboarding last month. It was awesome."

"It does sound like a lot of fun," Allie agreed.

"I can't wait to try it," Stephanie added. Everyone on the bus began talking about learning to snowboard.

Tweeeet!

"Uh, excuse me," she heard her father say, "but isn't snowboarding dangerous?"

CHAPTER
6

◆ ◂ ◗ ◆

The Flamingoes burst out laughing. Stephanie felt like hiding under her seat.

Mr. Merin grinned. "Well, snowboarding *can* be dangerous," he explained. "But we'll wear protective gear, of course."

"Oh. Okay, then," Danny said. He smiled and sat back down.

"Now, the most important thing is for everyone to break up into teams of four people," Mr. Merin announced. "Pick a name for your team, and let me know what it is. I'll make sure each team has the same number of kids," he added.

Allie and Darcy spun around in their seat to face Stephanie. They began tossing out team name suggestions.

"The Gliders?" Allie said.

Stephanie crinkled up her nose. "Nah. Too boring. What about the Ski Babes?"

Darcy made a face. "No. That sounds like something the Flamingoes would choose! How about something more action packed. Like Danger on the Slopes?"

"I like that," Michelle said.

Stephanie scoffed. "Oh, yeah, Dad will *really* like that name."

"Oh, right," Darcy said. "I forgot about your dad. We need something safe but jazzy."

"I've got it!" Allie said. "Snow Jazz!"

"Perfect! That's totally cool," Stephanie said.

"I love it," Darcy agreed.

"It's a great name!" Michelle said. "I can't wait to learn how to snowboard with you guys."

"No way, Michelle," Stephanie said. "I'm not having a little sister tag-along on my snowboard team."

Michelle pouted. "But I don't know anybody else here," she said. "I promise I won't get in your way."

"Forget it!" Stephanie shook her head.

"I'm telling Dad, then." Michelle started to stand.

Stephanie caught her sister's arm. "Wait!" Her

father had just made her promise to include Michelle. He'd have a fit if he heard Michelle complaining already.

"Just hang on a second, Michelle." Stephanie took a deep breath. "I, uh, changed my mind. You can be on our team. Okay?"

Michelle sat back down. "Really?"

"Really. But you're not an *official* member," Stephanie told her. "And don't ask millions of questions and bug me about everything."

Michelle held up two fingers. "Scout's honor," she promised.

Stephanie felt a little better. So maybe her trip *was* filled with family and Flamingoes. But a snowboarding race sounded awesome!

"All right!" Stephanie exclaimed. "Now, Darcy, I think you should give us a snowboarding lesson and—"

"Hey, Stephanie!" a voice suddenly called out from the back of the bus.

Stephanie rolled her eyes. Rene again. The trip had barely begun and Rene was already getting on her nerves.

"What do you want, Rene?" Stephanie called back.

"Is your pathetic little team going to enter the snowboarding race?" Rene asked.

"Why do you care?" Stephanie asked.

"I don't," Rene replied. "I'm just giving you some good advice—don't even bother entering. Because the Iced Flamingoes are going to win it."

"Iced Flamingoes? Great name," Stephanie said sarcastically.

"Oh, I suppose you have a better one?" Rene smirked.

"Snow Jazz *is* a great name," Stephanie called out.

Rene stood up and hurried to Stephanie's seat. She bent close to Stephanie and lowered her voice. "Anyway," she said, "how about a little bet?"

Stephanie stared at her suspiciously. "What are you talking about?"

Rene grinned. "If Snow Jazz does better in the snowboarding race, then the Iced Flamingoes will become your personal slaves back at school—for one whole day. But if *we* do better, you guys have to do what we say. For a whole day."

Stephanie's eyes widened. She glanced at Darcy and Allie. They seemed just as surprised as she was. Stephanie looked to the front of the bus to see if her father or Mr. Merin was listening. She knew they wouldn't approve of a bet like this. Luckily her dad and Mr. Merin were busy talking to the other chaperones. They didn't hear a word Rene and Stephanie said.

"I don't know," Stephanie said.

Then an image flashed across Stephanie's mind. Rene and the other Flamingoes were carrying her books to her locker. They were lugging her books to each class . . . even cutting her pizza for her in the cafeteria.

It couldn't get any cooler than that, Stephanie thought.

"What do you think, guys?" she whispered to Darcy and Allie.

"I think it would be a dream come true," Darcy said.

"I like it," Allie agreed.

"But Stephanie, Dad said—" Michelle began.

"Shush, Michelle!" Stephanie told her. "This is too cool," she whispered to her friends. "Can you imagine if we won?"

Allie frowned. "I don't know, Stephanie," she said. "Remember what happened the last time you took a bet?"

"Yeah. When you challenged me and Sara Allbright to a challenge tennis match," Darcy reminded her.

Stephanie made a face. "Oh, yeah. Right." Sara was a fantastic player. Stephanie was almost a beginner. Trying to beat Sara and Darcy at tennis had almost made Stephanie into a total physical wreck.

"But this is different!" Stephanie insisted. "Nobody here is a great snowboarder. You've seen Rene and the other Flamingoes during gym. They're pathetic. And Darcy can already snowboard. We could win this, guys."

"I guess," Allie said.

"I say go for it," Darcy put in.

"Right." Stephanie nodded. She turned to face Rene. And suddenly realized that all the kids in the back of the bus were listening.

"You've got a deal!" she told Rene.

Rene giggled. "Good luck—losers!" She headed back to her seat. A moment later all the Flamingoes burst out laughing.

"I *hate* that girl!" Stephanie told her friends. "We have to win this, you guys. We have to make Rene pay for all the obnoxious things she's ever said to me."

"And me," Allie agreed.

"Darcy, we're counting on you," Stephanie said. "You have exactly one day and one morning to turn us into the greatest snowboarders John Muir Middle School has ever seen!"

Tweeeeeeet!

Danny stood up at the front of the bus, signaling

for attention. "We'll be stopping for breakfast in a few minutes," he announced. "Please stay together so no one gets lost."

"Maybe that whistle will get lost," someone joked. Stephanie whirled around. Melody! She was grinning like crazy. And this time Rene was laughing along with her.

And I thought Melody might be different! Stephanie told herself. *No way! She's a Flamingo—just like the rest of them!*

The bus pulled into a diner parking lot. Stephanie told herself to ignore Rene and Melody. *I'll just think of something pleasant.*

The image of Rene lugging her books to class in front of the whole school came back into her head.

"Darcy, I can't wait for our first snowboarding lesson," she said.

They lined up to go into the diner. Darcy walked ahead of Stephanie and Allie.

"I can't wait, either," Darcy agreed. "Snowboarding is major fun! It's like surfing on snow! As soon as we get to the lodge, we'll sign out some snowboards. I'll have you 'surfin' flakes' in no time!"

Stephanie clasped her hands. "Cool! Rene won't know what hit her!"

"We'll be awesome," Allie agreed. "So what's the first thing we should know?"

"It's simple. Riding a snowboard is all a matter of shifting your weight," Darcy explained. She turned to glance at them as she walked down the steps of the bus. "You just have to . . . *aaaahhhhhhh!*"

Darcy missed the last step. Her feet flew out from under her. The next moment she was lying on the ground, clutching her ankle. "My ankle!" she cried. "I . . . I . . . think it's broken!"

CHAPTER
7

◆ ◀ ◢ ◆

"What happened? Is it broken?" Stephanie asked.

Darcy sat in a booth in the diner. Mr. Merin and Maria Cruz hovered over her. Mrs. Cruz was a registered nurse. She wrapped Darcy's ankle in an Ace bandage.

"No, it's not broken," Mr. Merin replied. "But it's a good thing Mrs. Cruz was along. I didn't know what to do."

"It's a bad sprain," Mrs. Cruz agreed. "But it will heal."

Darcy wiped a tear from her cheek. "It hurts, but I think I could walk on it," she said.

"None of that," Mrs. Cruz warned her. She frowned at Darcy. "You really should stay off that foot completely. At least until the swelling goes down."

Stephanie slid into the diner booth opposite Darcy. "When will that be?" she asked.

"It's hard to tell," Mrs. Cruz replied.

Stephanie looked at her in alarm. "But can she still ski?" she asked.

Mrs. Cruz shook her head. "Not this weekend. I wouldn't recommend it," she said.

"Darcy, would you like us to call your parents?" Mr. Merin asked. "Maybe they could drive up and take you home."

Darcy shook her head. "Oh, no. I'll be okay, really. I'll stay off it."

Allie brought a steaming cup of tea to the table. "Here, Darcy, just the way you like it. Milk and one sugar." She set the cup in front of Darcy.

"Thanks. I'm sorry, you guys," she added. "I guess I'm off the team, huh?"

"Don't worry about the team," Stephanie said. "Just try and get better."

"But what about the snowboarding lessons?" Darcy said. "If I can't walk, I can't snowboard. And that means I can't show you guys how to snowboard, either."

"Mr. Merin said we'd all get a lesson," Allie pointed out.

"Right!" Stephanie agreed, trying to act cheerful.

"But I was going to give you *extra* lessons," Darcy said. "I'm pretty much useless now. Plus Snow Jazz is one member short. How will you guys beat the Flamingoes now?"

Stephanie exchanged a glance with Allie. Darcy was right. There was no way they'd win the big race. Not with their star snowboarder out of commission. But neither of them had the heart to say so.

"It's not your fault, Darcy," Allie insisted. "Don't worry about us."

"We'll be fine," Stephanie added.

Yeah, fine, she thought. *Except that I don't even want to think about being a Flamingo slave for a day!*

Mr. Merin clapped for attention.

At least Dad didn't blow his whistle again, Stephanie told herself.

"Listen, everyone," Mr. Merin announced. "Darcy Powell has hurt her ankle. So we have to shuffle the teams around to make them more even." He studied his list of students.

"Mr. Merin!" Rene called out. "Don't forget that the Flamingoes all have to be on the same team."

Mr. Merin frowned. "This is a school event, Rene. I don't approve of private clubs. And you have the only girls team with five people. Everyone else has four. The teams should all be even."

"That's okay, Mr. Merin," Stephanie quickly added. "We don't need another person on our team! Darcy can still be in the sing-down and the scavenger hunt."

"She's right," Allie agreed. "And Darcy's ankle might be better by tomorrow's race."

Mr. Merin shook his head. "Sorry, girls. That wouldn't be fair to anyone."

"Right," Melody piped up. "And you know what they say, all's fair in love—and snowboard races." She chuckled. Rene shot her a dirty look.

Mr. Merin checked his list again. "Melody, you're on the Iced Flamingoes. Why don't you take Darcy's place?"

Melody's cheeks flushed. "Me?"

Stephanie, Allie, and Darcy exchanged horrified looks. Melody Kimball? A Flamingo? *On their team?*

Rene leaped to her feet. "Melody has to be on *our* team!" she cried.

"I don't think so," Mr. Merin answered calmly. "Melody, you'll take Darcy's place on Snow Jazz. Is that understood?"

Melody shot a quick glance at Rene, then answered, "Yes, Mr. Merin."

"But Mr. Merin!" Rene cried again. "That's really not fair!"

Stephanie couldn't believe what was happening. First her dad stuck her with Michelle. Now Mr. Merin stuck Melody on their team!

"Okay. Since the teams are all set, I can hand out your room assignments," Mr. Merin announced.

Stephanie's mouth fell open. "You don't mean that we're rooming together by teams?"

"Exactly." Mr. Merin nodded.

Stephanie felt sick to her stomach. That meant . . . that Melody was going to be *in their room!*

"When you're done eating, board the bus quickly," Mr. Merin finished. "We want a full day on those slopes!"

Everyone settled down to begin breakfast. When they were done, Stephanie and Allie helped Darcy hobble back to her seat on the bus.

"Tell me this isn't happening," Stephanie said. "Tell me we don't have to share a room with a Flamingo! How are the three of us going to have any fun? This is the worst possible news!"

"Uh-oh, Steph. I think the worst just got even worser," Allie said.

"What do you mean?" Stephanie asked.

"Look who's headed back this way . . . with her sleeping bag."

Stephanie turned around. Michelle was coming toward them. Her sleeping bag was tucked under her arm.

"Michelle, what are you doing with that sleeping bag?" Stephanie asked. "You won't need it until tonight."

"I didn't want to forget it when we unpacked in our room," Michelle answered.

"What do you mean, 'our room'?" Stephanie said. "You're sharing a room with Dad."

"Not anymore," Michelle told her. "You heard what Mr. Merin said. Teammates have to be roommates, too. Roomies . . . just like at home!" Michelle said happily. "This is going to be so great!"

Stephanie dropped her face into her hands and moaned. She couldn't believe her rotten luck. Surrounded by family and Flamingoes on the biggest school trip of the year.

Could things possibly get any worse?

They arrived at the lodge. Stephanie, Allie, and Michelle helped Darcy walk to their assigned room—room number 2. It was on the second floor of the lodge. All the girls were on the second floor, and all the boys were assigned to the third floor.

48

All the rooms were decorated the same way. They each had two large dressers, two bunk beds, and one single bed. Each room also had a large closet for storing ski equipment.

Stephanie dropped her things on the bottom of one bunk bed, and Darcy took the bottom of the other. Michelle chose the top bunk over Stephanie's. Allie took the top bunk over Darcy's.

Stephanie began to unpack.

"Why does Melody have to room with us?" she complained to Allie and Darcy. "Now we'll have to watch everything we say . . . every minute! For all we know, Melody will report every last word right to Rene!"

Still grumbling, she dumped the contents of her duffel bag into the top drawer of the dresser. Melody appeared at the door.

"Hey, guys!" Melody said. She was smiling.

Why is she so cheerful? Stephanie wondered. "Hey," she and the others muttered back.

Melody spread her sleeping bag over the single bed that was left.

"I'm really glad to be rooming with you guys," she said.

Stephanie glanced at her in surprise. "You are?" she asked.

Melody plopped down on the bed. "Definitely!

I am so glad I don't have to share a room with Rene and the others. I'm getting so sick of them!"

Stephanie, Darcy, and Allie exchanged doubtful glances.

"Especially Rene," Melody went on. "Did you ever notice how irritating her voice is?"

Stephanie's eyes widened. Had she ever noticed? She'd noticed the first moment she heard Rene's voice!

"And how bossy she is, too," Melody added. "She is the bossiest person on earth. She bosses the Flamingoes around. She bosses her sisters around. I've even seen her boss her *dog* around!"

Stephanie laughed and tried to cover it up by coughing.

"But we all thought you were friends with Rene," Allie pointed out.

Melody stood up and started to unpack. "I am . . . I mean, I *was*. When I first moved here last year, I didn't know anyone. Rene lived right next door. So we just started hanging around together. Then she got me into the Flamingoes."

Stephanie wondered what awful initiation Melody had to perform to be admitted into the Flamingoes. Stephanie would never trust the Flamingoes again.

"Don't you think it's a stupid club?" Melody

asked. "I mean, all that pink stuff—ugh! I *hate* pink! Rene loves it. She won't even wash her hair unless her shampoo is pink!"

Michelle giggled. "That's funny!" she said.

Stephanie frowned at Michelle, but Michelle ignored her. She smiled up at Melody and Melody smiled back.

"Rene's whole closet is filled with pink clothes. She even has three different pairs of pink sneakers!" Melody snickered. "You wouldn't catch me dead all decked out in pink. That's what Rene and I fight about most," she added. "Wearing pink. I refuse to do it."

"What about your new pink ski jacket?" Darcy asked.

Melody rolled her eyes. "Biggest mistake I ever made. I wish I didn't buy that ugly thing. But Rene said I couldn't ski with them unless I did." Melody pulled a blue-and-purple parka from her duffel bag and held it up. "But I have this one, too."

Darcy inspected the jacket. "Down filled," she commented. "Nice."

Melody smiled. "Thanks. Oh, and guess what? Want to hear the dumbest thing?"

"What?" Michelle asked. She sat on the bed next to Melody.

"Well, the Flamingoes aren't even allowed to

wear their new jackets again. Not until the big race on Sunday. Rene is so superstitious, she decided that wearing them before the race could be bad luck. So she's stashing all the jackets in the closet until Sunday." Melody laughed. "I think it's really because she finally realized how ugly they are!"

Stephanie laughed, too. She could never admit it to Allie and Darcy, but she kind of *liked* Melody. She actually seemed pretty cool. And she was definitely funny. Still, Stephanie reminded herself to be on guard. After all, no matter how nice Melody seemed, she was still a Flamingo. And not to be trusted.

"Why are you telling us all this?" Darcy asked.

"Yeah," Allie added. "Won't Rene kick you out of the club if she finds out what you said?"

Melody shrugged. "I couldn't care less," she said. "I told you, I'm sick of Rene bossing me around all the time. I'm sick of having to do everything together as a club. I'm sick of the color pink. Most of all, I'm sick of how Rene and the others talk about everybody behind their backs."

Darcy narrowed her eyes. "Is this an act, or are you telling us the truth?"

Melody straightened her shoulders. "I don't lie," she said quietly. "Anyway, who wants to go check out the showers?"

"I'll go!" Michelle leaped up and followed Melody out of the room. The showers were down at one end of the long hall.

"Hey, maybe Melody will actually be good for something," Stephanie said as soon as they had disappeared. "Like keeping Michelle out of my hair this weekend!"

"You mean you trust her?" Darcy asked.

"No! I mean I don't know," Stephanie answered.

"Well, I don't like the looks of it," Darcy replied. "Melody seems way too friendly. I mean, why was she going on and on about Rene like that?"

"Maybe she was waiting for us to say something bad," Allie suggested. "So that she could go back and tell Rene."

Darcy nodded. "Yeah, that's probably it. I'll bet she's not really thinking of leaving the Flamingoes at all."

Allie nodded thoughtfully. "That's probably exactly what's going on. It's all an act. I wouldn't put it past a Flamingo to pull a dirty trick like that!"

"But don't you think—" Stephanie began.

"Think what?" Darcy asked.

"Well, just that Melody is so friendly . . . and funny, too! Maybe we should give her a chance to—"

"Stephanie!" Darcy interrupted. "Do you re-

member who you're dealing with? A *Flamingo.*"
Darcy raised her eyebrows.

"She's right, Steph," Allie said. "Think about all
the times we were tricked by someone from that
awful club. And how nasty Rene was when Kyle
asked you out."

"She was pretty awful," Stephanie agreed.

"Let's make a pact," Darcy said. She put out her
hand. Immediately Allie put her hand on top of
Darcy's. Stephanie put her hand on top of Allie's.

"A pact that we won't say anything important
in front of Melody," Darcy finished.

"Especially anything about Rene Salter!" Allie
added. "Don't forget . . . Melody Kimball is a
Flamingo!"

"Right!" Stephanie agreed. "And you can never,
ever trust a Flamingo!"

CHAPTER
8

◆ ◀ ◢ ◆

Stephanie waved to Darcy through the big glass window at the lodge. Darcy sat inside, holding an ice pack on her ankle. Darcy forced a smile as she waved back.

Stephanie and Allie turned toward the slopes. Michelle followed after them with Melody.

"Poor Darcy," Allie said. "She must feel terrible. She must hate having to sit there and watch us have all the fun."

"Well, she might be able to get out some tomorrow," Stephanie said.

"I heard she's a pretty good skier. Is she?" Melody asked.

Stephanie rolled her eyes at Allie. They were barely out the door, and already Melody was digging for information about them! No doubt about it—the girl was bad news.

"Darcy? She's an okay skier," Stephanie replied. "Come on, Allie, let's find out where they're holding the snowboarding lesson."

"Oh, I heard the lesson is on the Deer Hill slope," Melody said. "I think it's over there." Melody pointed to the left.

Stephanie and Allie exchanged glances again.

"Um, actually, Melody," Stephanie said, "Allie and I were going to practice by ourselves today."

Melody's face fell. "Oh. I get it."

Stephanie felt a pang of guilt. If it were anyone else, she would agree that she was being too mean. *But you can't be too mean to a Flamingo*, she reminded herself. *Everyone knows that.*

"We'll see you at lunch, okay?" she added anyway.

Melody nodded. "Sure. I guess," she said quietly. She turned and plodded on ahead.

Stephanie and Allie waited a moment until Melody couldn't hear them anymore.

"Boy, that was close," Allie said.

"Why didn't you want Melody to go with us?" Michelle asked.

Stephanie put her hands on her hips. "Michelle,

remember what I told you about asking a million questions?"

"Right. Sorry," Michelle mumbled.

Michelle trudged through the snow behind Stephanie and Allie. They soon came to the Deer Hill slope. Mr. Merin and a ski instructor were already there in front of a crowd of kids. The instructor gave a short snowboarding demonstration. He showed them how to push off, how to stop, and how to shift their weight in order to steer the board.

Stephanie noticed Melody standing apart from everyone. Then she noticed Rene and the other Flamingoes.

"Melody was right," Stephanie whispered to Allie. "No pink parkas!"

Allie turned to stare at the Flamingoes. They wore an assortment of different-colored jackets. Allie giggled. "It's hard to recognize them without their pink on," she said.

"But it's not hard to avoid them," Stephanie answered. "And we *will* avoid them."

"Okay, people. Time for your first lesson in snowboarding," Mr. Merin announced.

Mr. Merin handed out one snowboard to each team. Snow Jazz received a wildly colored board. Stephanie lifted it to see how heavy it was.

"Not too heavy," she said. It was the first time she'd ever touched one before. "It looks just like a skateboard without the wheels," she noted.

"What did you think it looked like?" Michelle asked.

Stephanie ignored her. "Anyway, do you want to go first, Allie?"

Allie shook her head. "No . . . you'd better."

"I'll go first!" Michelle cried. "Can I? Can I?"

Stephanie took a deep breath. "Listen, Michelle. There's only one reason I'm letting you hang out with us. Because Dad is making me. But if you keep driving me nuts, you can forget about being in Snow Jazz at all!"

Michelle pursed her lips together and frowned.

"Got it?" Stephanie asked.

"Got it," Michelle repeated.

Stephanie practiced first. Then she handed the snowboard to Allie for a turn. When Allie was finished, she handed it back to Stephanie.

After a few more tries Stephanie finally let Michelle have a turn.

After all, Michelle is an unofficial member of Snow Jazz. She has to know the basics, she figured.

Stephanie watched as Michelle climbed onto the snowboard and began to coast smoothly down the hill.

58

"She's pretty good," Allie said. "Especially for her very first time."

Stephanie shrugged. "It's probably because she's lighter than us," she replied.

When Michelle trudged back up the hill, she was all smiles. "How did I do?" she asked.

Stephanie took the board back. "You seemed a little shaky," she told her. "Come on. Let's find somewhere else to practice. I want to try that dismount again."

They found a spot close to the bottom of the slope. "We can practice by ourselves here," Stephanie said.

"Not exactly," Allie told her. "Look who's here."

Stephanie noticed Kyle Sullivan and his team, the Downhill Dudes, practicing nearby.

"Oh. Kyle looks pretty cute in his parka," Stephanie admitted. She bent to tighten her boot.

"You're not the only one who thinks so. Look who's up to her old tricks again," Allie whispered in Stephanie's ear.

Stephanie turned. Rene ran up to Kyle. She watched as Rene put her hand on Kyle's shoulder and gazed into his eyes.

"Yuck! Why is he even talking to her?" Stephanie asked.

"Why is who talking to who?" Michelle asked.

"Nobody," Stephanie replied. She turned to Allie. "He told me he thought Rene was stuck up," she whispered.

"Do you mean Kyle?" Michelle asked.

Stephanie's face reddened. "Michelle! Stop eavesdropping! This is a private conversation!"

Allie giggled. "Rene isn't even trying to practice. None of the Flamingoes are. They're all more interested in flirting."

The Flamingoes were all grouped around the Downhill Dudes now. Mary and Julie started a snowball fight. The boys pelted them with snow and they ran away, screeching as if they were afraid.

"Those Flamingoes are so lame," Stephanie said. "Let them flirt. We'll practice. Then we'll definitely beat them tomorrow!"

Stephanie climbed onto the board and pushed off. She meant to go to her right, but the board veered left—right toward Kyle and his friends.

Stephanie tried to look casual. She would just coast past them and wave. The board swerved and suddenly she found herself riding with only one foot on the board! Her other foot trailed behind her. She tried to catch her balance. But it was hopeless.

"Oh, no—" A second later she was flat on her

face. When she pulled her face out of the snow, Rene was standing a few feet away.

"Developing a new sport, Stephanie?" Rene called loudly. "Like *spaz*boarding?"

Everyone within earshot began to laugh. Including Kyle!

"How could she invent it?" Melody asked. "You already won the gold medal in it!"

Everyone laughed again. Everyone but Rene. Her mouth hung open in shock. Stephanie pulled herself up and brushed the snow off her jacket. She wished she had thought of something clever to say back to Rene. But she was too embarrassed to think straight. Melody had beaten her to it— again!

Tweeeet! Tweeeet!

Everyone was still laughing when Stephanie's father pushed his way through the crowd. A ski patrol member was right behind him.

"Stephanie! Are you okay, honey?" he asked. "Do you need a doctor?"

Stephanie's face turned immediately red again. "No, Dad. I'm *fine*."

"It's okay!" Danny called to the ski patrol. "She's fine! Cancel the first-aid mobile unit!"

Stephanie heard a few kids snicker. She wished

she could bury herself in the snow. "Dad!" she whispered. "You're embarrassing me!"

Danny seemed hurt. "I'm sorry, Steph. I was just a little worried, that's all."

"Well, stop worrying," Stephanie told him. She tucked the snowboard under her arm. "Come on," she told Allie and Michelle. "Let's get back to practice!"

Stephanie balanced on the snowboard again.

"Wait, Stephanie," Michelle told her. "The ski instructor said to lean forward. And he said to keep your weight behind you."

"I know, Michelle!" Stephanie snapped. "I was there, too, remember? That's what I've been trying to do!"

"But you did it all wrong. That's why you fell," Michelle pointed out.

"So I'll do better this time. So keep quiet," Stephanie snapped.

"I was only trying to help!" Michelle replied.

"Well, I don't need any help," Stephanie shot back. "I can do this! I'm not a total spaz, you know!"

"Hey! You guys need some help?"

Stephanie, Allie, and Michelle looked up to see Melody standing in front of them, holding a snowboard.

"Because I can show you how to—"

"No!" Stephanie insisted. "I . . . *we* don't need any help! Allie, let's practice over there," she said, pointing across the slope. "Where we can get some privacy."

Allie followed her to the other side of the slope. Stephanie dropped the snowboard onto the ground. She saw that Michelle had stayed behind with Melody.

Fine with me! Stephanie thought.

Stephanie stepped onto the snowboard—and immediately slipped off again.

"I just don't get it!" she complained in frustration. "I'm usually pretty athletic, right, Allie? Why can't I do this right?"

"You're letting Michelle and the Flamingoes distract you, Steph," Allie said. "Try not to think about them."

"You're right. I'm not concentrating," Stephanie said. "But how can I? Michelle is being a pest, and Melody keeps popping up all over the place."

A loud squeal sounded from the bottom of the slope. It was Rene, flirting with Kyle again.

Stephanie was so angry, she thought her blood was going to boil. "Rene is so pathetic! Look at her! She's practically hanging all over Kyle!"

"Stephanie—you're doing it again," Allie said.

"Stop thinking about Rene and Kyle . . . and Michelle and Melody . . . and concentrate!"

"Okay! You're right!"

Allie pointed to the bottom of the slope. "I'll go down there. You ride down to me. Try to keep to a straight path."

Stephanie nodded. She and Allie spent the next half hour taking turns. Stephanie fell nearly every time, but each ride made her feel less shaky.

"That was a good one!" Allie cried excitedly. "Try it again, Steph. Without looking down at the ground."

Stephanie climbed back up the slope. She pointed the snowboard right toward Allie. Then she heard Rene and Kyle, laughing and joking around again.

I'm going to show them both that I'm not a spaz, she told herself.

She tried to remember what the instructor had said—something about shifting her weight. She shifted her weight back. Suddenly she was soaring down the slope. The board was going a lot faster than she thought it should. There was a bright orange cone at the bottom of the slope. At the rate she was going, she'd smash into it for sure!

Stephanie shifted her weight from one leg to the

other, trying to steer to the right of the cone. The board veered left instead. And it flew faster than before.

Stephanie gulped. She was heading right toward the orange cone. And she couldn't remember how to stop!

CHAPTER
9

◆ ◂ ◆ ◆

"Help!" Stephanie screamed.

She smashed into the cone, tumbled off her snowboard, and landed flat on her back.

"Wait!" Rene called out loudly. "Which orange blob is the cone and which is Stephanie Tanner?"

Stephanie sat up. Rene was pointing at her. Mary, Julie, and Alyssa were laughing out loud. So were the Downhill Dudes.

Tweeeet!

Her whistle-blowing father appeared, tweeting furiously.

Stephanie felt her cheeks flush red. *Talk about embarrassing!* she thought, cringing.

"Okay, everyone! Back away!" Danny bent over Stephanie. "Sweetheart, are you okay?"

"I'm fine," she whispered back. "Stop it! You're embarrassing me again!"

Danny tried to help her stand.

"I can get up by myself," she told him, blushing furiously.

"Okay, then." Danny took off, whistling at another fallen snowboarder.

Stephanie pulled herself up. That last fall had hurt!

"Maybe you should take up a safer snow sport," Rene shouted to her. "Like shoveling!"

Allie hurried over to Stephanie. "Don't listen to her, Steph. Do you need help walking?"

"We can help." Melody and Michelle raced to Stephanie's side. They threw their arms around her back and shoulders, trying to help. Stephanie pulled away.

"I said I can walk by myself! Please, could everyone just leave me alone?"

"Need some help, Steph?" someone else asked.

Stephanie was about to snap back when she realized it was Kyle. He grinned at her and brushed back a wave of hair that fell over his forehead. She felt a little twinge. He *did* have an adorable smile. And those deep, brown eyes—

"Oh, hi, Kyle," she said, forcing herself to laugh. "I'm fine! Really. Just a little, uh, embarrassed, that's all." She sighed. "Okay . . . mortified is more like it."

Kyle grinned. "Nah, don't be embarrassed," he said gently. "Everyone falls on the slopes."

"Not as much as me," she joked.

Kyle shrugged. "It wasn't as bad as you think."

Stephanie laughed for real this time. "Are you crazy? I made a complete fool of myself in front of everyone!" she replied. "They'll never let me hear the end of it."

Kyle made a face. "Oh, everyone will forget about it in five minutes," he assured her.

Stephanie shook he head. "I don't know. . . ."

"Listen, I know what it's like to be *really* embarrassed," Kyle insisted. "This is nothing! When I was little, all the kids used to call me—" He paused and flushed.

"What did they call you?" Stephanie asked.

"You know, I swore I'd never tell another living soul. I can't even believe I said this much!"

"I won't tell anyone," Stephanie said.

Kyle glanced around to see if anyone was listening. He leaned close to Stephanie. "Promise. Swear you won't tell anyone else, ever," he said.

Stephanie nodded. "Promise. It never leaves this slope."

"Okay, then, here goes." Kyle took a deep breath. "They called me—Rufus the Dufus."

Stephanie gazed at Kyle in amazement. "Why?" she asked.

"Because my middle name . . . is Rufus." Kyle flushed even more.

Stephanie laughed. "Rufus?" she said. "Are you kidding? That's hysterical!"

"No, I'm not kidding. Let me tell you—*that* was embarrassing!" Kyle said.

Stephanie tried to stop laughing. But she couldn't.

"And thanks for being so understanding," Kyle added sarcastically.

"Oh, I didn't mean to laugh like that, Kyle. I was, uh, just surprised, that's all. I've never heard that name before."

"It's for my great-grandfather, Rufus Sullivan," he explained. "I used to get teased about it so much. I haven't told anyone about it since kindergarten."

"Well, don't worry, Kyle," Stephanie said sincerely. "Your secret is safe with me. And thanks. It was sweet of you to try to make me feel better."

To Stephanie's surprise, it was working, too. Aside from a few aches and pains, she was feeling pretty good.

Stephanie leaned over to pick up her snowboard. When she straightened up, she caught Rene staring right at her and Kyle. Stephanie could tell the Flamingo was steaming with jealousy.

Let me give you something better to stare at, Stephanie thought. *Hey, Rene! Get a load of this!*

"Uh, Kyle, could you help me to that bench over there?" Stephanie asked sweetly. She pointed to a bench at the bottom of the slope. It was there so people could sit and adjust their ski boots. "I really need to sit down."

"Sure, Steph." Kyle put his arm around her waist. He helped her walk to the bench. Stephanie made sure that she clung to him extra tightly.

"Thanks, Kyle," Stephanie said.

"No problem." Kyle gave her a little wave. He hurried back to his buddies. Immediately Allie, Melody, and Michelle raced over to her.

"Stephanie, you should have seen the look on Rene's face when she saw you with Kyle," Allie exclaimed. "Talk about jealous!"

Stephanie beamed.

"Are you guys going together again?" Melody asked.

Stephanie stared at Melody. "Going out? We're not going out."

"But you used to go out with him, right?" Michelle asked. "Weren't you just talking about that time you had a big crush on him?"

"Michelle!" Stephanie exclaimed. "Will you be quiet!" She blinked up at Melody. "No, Kyle and I are just friends," she explained.

"That's weird," Melody said. "Because Rene said you had a big crush on Kyle and that he didn't like you."

Stephanie stared at Melody in shock. "Where did Rene hear *that?* It isn't true—not at all! Kyle *did* like me! He asked me out on a date. No, *two* dates," she said. "So that proves it. *He* liked *me!*"

"Really?" Melody shrugged. "That's not what I heard. I don't think Rene would make things up. I—"

"Listen to me, Melody," Stephanie interrupted. "I do not and have never had a crush on Kyle Rufus Sullivan!"

Melody laughed. "Rufus?" she said. "Kyle's middle name is Rufus?"

Stephanie clapped her hands over her mouth. *What have I done!*

She had just promised Kyle she wouldn't tell another living soul about his middle name. And she'd already blurted it out! To Melody—a Flamingo!

Stephanie grabbed Melody's arm. "Listen, Melody! You can't tell anyone what I just said!"

Melody chuckled. "What kind of a name is Rufus?"

"Melody! Swear you won't tell!" Stephanie pleaded. "Please, please, please! I won't leave you alone until you promise."

"Okay, okay!" Melody said. "I won't tell."

"Won't tell what?" a voice asked.

Stephanie whirled around.

Alyssa Norman and Julie Chu were standing right behind her. "Some juicy gossip, Stephanie?" Julie asked. She and Alyssa grinned at each other. Stephanie gulped nervously. Had they heard?

"Nothing," Stephanie mumbled. She handed the snowboard to Michelle. "Here. Practice all you want. I'm going to see Darcy," she announced.

"I'll come with you," Allie said. She followed Stephanie toward the lodge.

"This is the worst day of my life," Stephanie said as they walked.

"Oh, Steph. Don't you think you're overreacting?" Allie asked.

"I've just been embarrassed in front of the whole school," Stephanie cried. "That's not overreacting."

"It wasn't so bad, Steph. And anyway, you also

just made Rene jealous. Didn't you catch the look on her face? It was great!"

"Yeah, that part was pretty great." She frowned. "But I just made a humongous mistake, Al," she added.

"What?"

"Kyle told me to keep his middle name a secret. And I blurted it out in front of Melody. What if she tells Rene? Kyle will kill me!"

"Maybe she won't tell," Allie said. "Or—" Allie stopped talking. "Hey! Did you see that?" she asked.

Stephanie looked over her shoulder. "No, what?"

Allie pointed to a group of kids who were staring at them. "I think they were laughing at us."

"No big surprise there, Al. I just made history tumbling down the mountain, remember?" Stephanie ducked her head.

Allie shrugged. They passed another group of kids. And heard more giggles. Two kids pointed right at Stephanie.

"They can't still be laughing about that. Tons of kids fell on the slopes today." Allie shook her head. "No. Something else is going on. But what?"

"I don't know. Let's just get to the lodge so this

awful morning can be over," Stephanie said. She turned to go into the lodge. Allie let out a gasp.

"Uh-oh!" she said.

"What? What is it?" Stephanie demanded.

Allie reached around and pulled something off the back of Stephanie's jacket. "No wonder everyone is laughing." She held up a big piece of paper. "It's a sign. See?"

Stephanie stared. Scrawled across the paper were big, black letters:

STEPHANIE TANNER: SNOW SPAZ!!

Stephanie snatched the sign from Allie and crumpled it up. "Who did this?" she demanded.

"Rene?" Allie suggested.

Stephanie shook her head. "Couldn't be. I never got close enough to her. But I'll bet that it was one of the other Flamingoes."

Just then Melody, Alyssa, and Julie walked by on their way to the lodge. They pointed at Stephanie and snickered.

Stephanie tightened her fist around the crumpled sign. "That's it!" she exclaimed to Allie.

"What?" Allie asked.

"It's so obvious," Stephanie said. "Who was right there when I fell? Who kept trying to help me up, pretending to be friendly? Who touched my back a couple of times?"

"I don't know," Allie said in confusion. 'There were lots of people around."

"But only one could be this sneaky," Stephanie said. "There's only one person who could have done it. It was Melody!"

CHAPTER
10

♦ ◄ ◆ ♦

"Wait till I tell Darcy what Melody did *this* time," Stephanie snapped.

She rushed into the lodge. Allie hurried after her. They found Darcy sitting in her place at the big window, still holding an ice pack on her ankle.

"What's going on?" Darcy asked. "I saw everyone outside laughing and pointing at you, Stephanie."

Stephanie groaned. "This morning was a total nightmare!"

"Plus our snowboarding is pretty awful," Allie told her.

Stephanie and Allie quickly told Darcy everything that had happened that morning.

"Is your ankle any better?" Stephanie asked Darcy. "Will you be back on the team tomorrow?"

"I doubt it," Darcy said. She rose from her chair. "It doesn't hurt as much as before. But it's still pretty swollen."

Stephanie and Allie helped Darcy into the cafeteria for lunch. They found a table in the section of the room that was roped off for kids on the school trip.

Darcy lowered herself into her chair. "I'm sorry about this morning, you guys," she said. "I thought Melody was acting way too nice. Boy, those Flamingoes are such phonies!"

"Well, I'm not falling for any more of their tricks," Stephanie said. "I'm going to nail all the Flamingoes. And then kick Melody out of our room—and off our team!"

"Hey, guys." Michelle hurried to their table. She pulled out an empty chair and sat down. "Where did you go? I looked everywhere for you. Melody just showed me how to—"

"Don't mention that girl's name," Stephanie said.

Michelle seemed confused. "Who, Melody?"

"That's right," Stephanie said. "She's the enemy!"

"But I thought you liked her," Michelle said.

"She's a Flamingo," Stephanie replied. "And that's bad news."

Michelle shrugged. "Well, I think she's pretty nice. She showed me how to make a turn on the snowboard. And after lunch she's going to teach me how to ski."

Stephanie frowned. "Really? Why is Melody getting all chummy with you?"

"Maybe she likes me," Michelle said.

Stephanie laughed out loud. "No way, Michelle!" She leaned close to her little sister. "I don't want you talking to her, okay? Or hanging around with her, either."

Michelle stared down at her lunch plate. "But—"

"Michelle, if you hang around with Melody, then you can't hang around with us. Got it?" Stephanie asked.

Michelle hesitated. "Well, yeah, okay," she answered.

"Good," Stephanie said. Then she turned back to Allie and Darcy. "Now, what will we do about this snowboarding thing? We'll never beat the Flamingoes in the race tomorrow with the way we're snowboarding. We need major help. Especially if Darcy isn't better by tomorrow."

Michelle looked up. "I know. You could—"

"Shhh," Stephanie ordered. "This is important."

Darcy motioned her friends closer and lowered her voice. "I have an idea," she said. "I found out that you could take a private snowboarding lesson! Two of the instructors give them every morning. But you have to get up really early or else their classes fill up."

Stephanie brightened. "What an excellent idea!" She looked at Allie, who seemed just as pleased.

"Can I come, too?" Michelle asked.

Stephanie rolled her eyes. "Oh, okay, Michelle," she said impatiently. "Just stop bothering me."

"Well, a private lesson should do the trick," Allie said. "We all saw how the Flamingoes hardly practiced skiing or snowboarding all morning, right?"

"Yeah, I noticed that, too," Darcy said.

"Okay, then," Stephanie said. "If we take an extra lesson, we'll have a pretty good chance of beating them tomorrow."

Stephanie sat back in her chair. "Just think about it, you guys. Imagine us winning the race! This time on Monday the Flamingoes could be serving us lunch—in front of the whole school!"

Allie giggled. "I'd like Mary Kelly to be my own personal slave," she said. "Once I asked her if I could borrow a pen in the middle of a test, and

Mary told the teacher I was cheating off her! I almost got in really big trouble."

"That is so low," Darcy remarked.

"Yeah. If we win, I'll make Mary sharpen my pencils, fill my juice glass at lunch, and even brush my hair," Allie said.

"Imagine snobby Mary brushing your hair!" Stephanie giggled. "You should make her clean your hairbrush when she's done!"

"Yeah, and I'd make Alyssa and Julie carry my books from class to class," Darcy said. "And I just happen to need all my heaviest textbooks on Monday!"

"Just leave Rene and Melody for me," Stephanie said. "I'll plan a whole day of humiliation for them. And I'll make sure the photographer from the *Scribe* captures all these special moments on film for the school paper."

Darcy and Allie both slapped her high fives.

"Hey, look at that!" Allie pointed to a table across the room. "Remember how Melody said she was sick of the Flamingoes?"

Stephanie and Darcy turned. Melody was sitting at a round table with Rene, Alyssa, Julie, and Mary. They were huddled over their lunch trays, whispering.

"She doesn't look very sick right now," Stephanie said.

Stephanie had turned back to her food when she noticed Kyle and his friends hurrying into their section of the cafeteria.

Kyle was laughing and his cheeks were flushed. Stephanie thought he looked cuter than ever.

Suddenly everyone in their part of the cafeteria fell silent. Then a couple of kids began to chant: *"Rufus. Rufus."*

More kids joined in. Soon their whole section of the room was clapping and chanting: "Rufus! Rufus!"

"Oh, no!" Stephanie cried in horror.

"Rufus? What does that mean, anyway?" Darcy wondered.

"Don't ask!" Stephanie moaned.

Across the room Kyle's face flushed even redder—in embarrassment. For a moment he looked as if he wanted to run. Then he caught Stephanie's eye. He strode right over to her table.

"Thanks a lot, *friend*," he said sarcastically.

Stephanie felt her own cheeks grow hot. "But Kyle. I . . . I . . ." She didn't know what to say.

"I can't believe you told!" Kyle exclaimed. "You promised not to!" Kyle turned and stormed out of the cafeteria. Stephanie had never seen him so mad.

"What is going on?" Darcy demanded.

"Rufus is Kyle's middle name," Stephanie explained. "He told me this morning. And I . . . I let it slip," she admitted. "To Melody! But she promised she'd never tell anyone!"

Darcy, Allie, and Michelle stared at her. "You trusted a Flamingo?" Darcy asked.

Stephanie swallowed hard. "I feel awful," she whispered. "I never meant for this to happen. Never!"

How could she have told Melody about Kyle's middle name? Melody must have told Rene right away. And now the whole school knew!

"Kyle will never forgive me." Stephanie moaned. "I can't believe Melody did this to me!" she cried. "She really got me this time. But I know one thing—" Stephanie paused. "I'll never trust that Flamingo again!"

CHAPTER
11

◆ ◂ ▸ ◆

For two solid hours after lunch Stephanie and Allie practiced snowboarding—alone. They were determined to learn everything they needed to know to win the big race.

"We're getting better, don't you think?" Allie finally asked.

Stephanie brushed snow off her parka and jeans. "Better. But not quite good enough," she replied.

Allie checked her watch. "Hey, it's almost four o'clock. We have to get back for the sing-down."

"Great," Stephanie said. "I need a break from falling down. Besides, I love sing-downs!"

They hurried back to the lodge. Everyone was gathered in the social hall. Stephanie, Allie, and

Darcy each grabbed a pad of paper and a pen and took a spot on the floor. The teams all sat together.

"Okay, everyone." Mr. Merin called the room to order. "Let's review the rules. I'll call out a topic— a color, a place, or a person's name. You put your heads together as a team and write down song titles that use that word. But remember, when it's your turn, you have to sing the titles."

"We can win this—no problem," Stephanie said. She winked at Allie and Darcy. They all knew Snow Jazz had an advantage: Allie knew almost every song ever written, thanks to her parents' enormous music collection.

Michelle plopped down next to Stephanie, squeezing between her and Allie. "I love sing-downs," she gushed. "We had them in day camp all the time."

Stephanie exchanged a look of surprise with Darcy and Allie. "Uh, what do you think you're doing, Michelle?"

Michelle stared back in confusion. "I'm going to be in the sing-down," she said. "I'm on the Snow Jazz team. Unofficially."

Darcy and Allie sighed. So did Stephanie. Did Michelle have to tag along for every minute of the trip?

Stephanie stood up and searched the room for

her father. She spotted him handing out pens and paper. Stephanie hurried over.

"Uh, Dad?" she called. "Can I ask you something?"

Danny smiled. "Hey, Steph. How's it going? Having fun?"

Stephanie nodded. "Yeah, but does Michelle have to be in the sing-down with us? I mean, can't I do one thing this weekend without her?"

Danny frowned. "Stephanie, Michelle doesn't know anybody else here. It wouldn't be nice to exclude her."

"But she's been hanging around me all day," Stephanie complained.

"I know it's hard for you, Steph," Danny told her. "But your sister is here, and that's that. You'll just have to deal with it."

Stephanie marched back to her team. *Some trip this is turning out to be!* she thought.

Stephanie stopped in shock. Melody was sitting next to Michelle.

"What are you doing here?" Stephanie demanded.

Melody glanced up, looking surprised. "I'm here for the sing-down," she replied. "I'm a member of Snow Jazz, remember?"

Stephanie glanced at Darcy and Allie.

"She's right," Allie said. "Mr. Merin told her to be on our team." Allie shrugged helplessly.

Stephanie sat down in a huff. "I guess you made up with Rene and the others," she said.

Melody made a face. "Not exactly. I mean, I still can't stand Rene. She makes me sick. But Alyssa's pretty nice once you get to know her."

"We saw you sitting with them at lunch," Darcy said. "You didn't seem to be so sick of Rene."

Melody's eyes widened. "It's not what you think," she protested. "I told you. I don't want to be in the Flamingoes anymore. That's the truth."

"Is it?" Stephanie asked. "Then tell me how everyone knew Kyle's middle name. I mentioned it in front of you, and next thing I know, the whole school is teasing him. You promised not to tell anyone!"

"I didn't tell," Melody insisted.

Before Stephanie could say another word, Mr. Merin called for quiet.

"Okay, everyone. Time to begin your lists. The first topic is *cry*. You've got five minutes to write down all the songs you know with the word *cry* in the title. Good luck."

Stephanie forgot about Melody and began scribbling furiously. " 'Don't Cry for Me, Argentina,' " she said.

" 'Big Girls Don't Cry,' " Melody suggested.

Stephanie ignored her. " 'Let Her Cry,' " she added.

Allie scrunched up her nose. "Who sings that?"

"Hootie and the Blowfish," Melody explained. "I love them."

Without thinking, Stephanie smiled. "Me too. They're excellent." Then she remembered who she was talking to. "I mean, they're okay sometimes."

Mr. Merin called out more topics. The teams made more lists. Finally he called out the last topic: *"Yellow."* "Do we have 'Follow the Yellow Brick Road'?" Allie asked.

Stephanie nodded. "Got it."

"And 'Yellow Submarine'?" Darcy asked.

Stephanie nodded again.

"What about 'Yellow Rose in the Morning'?" Michelle asked.

"That's not the name of the song," Stephanie said.

"Sure, it is," Michelle insisted. She began to sing.

Stephanie held up her hand. "Michelle. I know the song you mean. But that's not the name of it."

Michelle put her hands on her hips. "It is, too," she insisted.

"I think she's right," Melody remarked.

"I don't think so," Darcy told her.

"Anyway, we didn't ask you," Stephanie pointed out.

"It *is* the name," Michelle insisted again. "Joey sings that song all the time."

"Michelle, it's not the name," Stephanie snapped.

"Is, too."

"Well, I'm team captain, and I'm not writing it down," Stephanie declared.

Michelle sat back angrily. "Fine! Don't listen," she said.

"Come on, guys, think," Stephanie said to the others. "We're running out of time."

But no one could think of another song that had the word *yellow* in it. Stephanie tapped her pen against her chin.

"I've got it!" she cried. "In a Yellow Mood," she whispered. It's a song my uncle Jesse recorded with his band last year."

Allie smiled. "Perfect! No one else will know that song."

"We all have to sing it, though," Darcy said. "And I don't know how it goes."

Stephanie quietly sang two lines of the chorus for them so they'd know the words and the melody.

"Time's up," Mr. Merin announced. "There's

cocoa set up for everyone in the hall. Let's take a ten-minute break, then come back and sing! Don't forget to guard your answers. We don't want any cheating."

"You can say that again," Stephanie murmured. She put down the song list, making sure the answers were hidden. Then she jumped up. She and Allie helped Darcy to stand.

"Aren't you coming, Michelle?" Allie asked.

"No." Michelle stubbornly shook her head.

"She's still mad about the song, I guess," Stephanie told her friends. "Just ignore her." She, Allie, and Darcy hurried into the hall. They helped themselves to cocoa and snacks.

When they returned to the main room, Stephanie's jaw dropped. "I don't believe it!" she exclaimed. She pointed across the room.

Melody was talking to Rene and the Flamingoes!

"Oh, yeah," Darcy said sarcastically, "she is really sick of Rene."

"For someone who's planning to quit the Flamingoes, she's spending an awful lot of time with them," Allie agreed.

"Hey, Stephanie," Darcy said suddenly, "did you leave our list just sitting here this way?"

Stephanie glanced down. Their song list was

faceup on the floor. Anyone could read their answers!

"Michelle was here," Stephanie said. "I thought she'd guard the list while we were gone. Where did she go, anyway?"

"I don't know. I just hope no one saw our list," Darcy said.

It was time to continue the sing-down. Michelle hurried to take her place on the floor.

"Michelle, you left our list lying faceup," Stephanie complained.

"Sorry." Michelle shrugged.

"Well, you might have just cost us the game," Stephanie began. She would have said more, but Melody came back to the group. Stephanie, Darcy, and Allie exchanged knowing glances.

"The first topic is *cry*," Mr. Merin announced. "Iced Flamingoes . . . you're first."

Rene and her team sang, *"Big girls don't cry. Big girls don't cry. Bi-ig girls don't cry-aye-aye. They don't cry."*

They sounded so awful that everyone laughed.

One point to the Iced Flamingoes," Mr. Merlin said. "Now, all you teams who also had that song on your lists have to cross it off."

There was a loud groan from half the teams in the room. Then it was Snow Jazz's turn.

Stephanie whispered, "One, two, three, sing!"

She, Melody, Allie, and Michelle began to sing "Let Her Cry" as loudly as they could. But Darcy sang "Don't Cry for Me, Argentina."

There were snickers and cackles of laughter. Darcy flushed. She couldn't carry a tune to save her life. Stephanie started giggling, and the others joined in. Finally Darcy burst out laughing, too.

They managed to keep straight faces as they finished the song. The sing-down continued. Finally they came to the last topic—*yellow.*

Mr. Merin clapped for quiet. "This is it, people!" he announced. "Four teams are tied for first place. Whoever wins this category wins the sing-down!"

The room hushed. "The Iced Flamingoes will go first," Mr. Merin said.

The Iced Flamingoes sprang up and sang two lines from the Beatles' song "Yellow Submarine."

Stephanie groaned. "Cross that one off our list," she whispered.

The Frosty Fighters were next. They began to sing "Yellow Rose in the Morning."

Michelle shot Stephanie a triumphant look. "See! I told you that was the title of that song."

Stephanie ignored her.

Next the Sassy Skiers sang "The Yellow Rose of Texas."

Then it was time for Snow Jazz. Stephanie leaped up and led the team in a chorus of the Elton John song "Goodbye Yellow Brick Road."

"That's one additional point for each team," Mr. Merin announced. "We're still tied. So let's move right into round two. The topic is still *yellow*. The first team to stump the others wins. Good luck!"

Stephanie checked her team list. They had one last song left: "In a Yellow Mood." If the other teams dropped out in this round, then Snow Jazz could sneak in with "In a Yellow Mood" and win.

"The Iced Flamingoes are first," Mr. Merin said.

"No problem," Rene called out. "Ready, guys?" The Iced Flamingoes jumped to their feet. They began to sing "In a Yellow Mood."

"What . . . ?" Stephanie's jaw nearly hit the floor. "How could they possibly know Uncle Jesse's song?"

Mr. Merin called for silence. "How about it, Frosty Fighters? Do you have another *yellow* song?"

The Frosty Fighters passed. So did the Sassy Skiers.

"Snow Jazz?" Mr. Merin asked.

"Uh, we had, uh, the same song," Stephanie stammered. " 'In a Yellow Mood.' "

"Then we have a winner!" Mr. Merin shouted. "Iced Flamingoes!"

There was a burst of good-natured applause. Stephanie blinked in astonishment. "They win? The Flamingoes win?" Stephanie almost choked in disappointment.

Darcy and Allie looked shocked.

"I can't believe it!" Melody said. "Rene and those guys probably cheated." She laughed. Then she realized no one was laughing with her.

"*You'd* know that better than anyone," Stephanie told her. "Especially since *you* helped them cheat."

Melody's eyes widened. "Who, me?" she asked. "I didn't help them."

"Oh, no?" Stephanie demanded. "Then how did they know about 'In a Yellow Mood'? My uncle Jesse wrote that song. No one but us knew it."

"Plus we all saw you talking to Rene during the snack break," Darcy added.

"Admit it, Melody," Allie added. "It sure looks like you cheated to help them win."

Melody stood up. "You're right." she replied. "I *was* talking to Rene during the break. But I was telling her I'm quitting the Flamingoes."

"We don't believe you," Stephanie told her. "We think you're still friends with Rene and the other

Flamingoes. In fact, we think you're spying for them. We want you off the team. Now."

"I'm not a spy!" Melody exclaimed. "Honest."

"Sorry," Darcy replied. Stephanie shrugged. Allie stared at the floor.

Melody looked as though she might cry. Instead she picked up her ski parka and stomped out of the room.

"Boy, she seemed so *upset*," Allie remarked. "I don't suppose . . . do you think, uh, maybe . . . she might be telling the truth?"

Stephanie gaped at Allie in surprise. "You're sticking up for Melody? How else could the Flamingoes have won? She *had* to tell them our answers."

Darcy agreed. "Yeah. It's too much of a coincidence."

"And what about all that other stuff?" Stephanie reminded her. "The nasty sign on my back? And telling everyone about Kyle's middle name?"

Darcy nodded. "Melody was always around when all those things happened."

"I guess so," Allie said.

Darcy stretched. "Well, I'm going to ice my ankle some more. It's feeling much better now. I may even be able to hit the slopes tomorrow."

"All right!" Stephanie cheered. "That would be awesome, Darcy. We really need you."

"That's great, Darcy," Allie said. She glanced at her watch. "Listen, maybe Steph and I should squeeze in a little more snowboarding practice before dinner. Then let's meet in the dining room. Whoever gets there first save a table."

"And make sure it only has three chairs," Stephanie added. "I don't want any spies as dinner guests!"

CHAPTER
12

♦ ◀ ▶ ♦

"So, snowboarders, how did it go?" Darcy asked.

Stephanie limped into the lodge dining room. Allie followed, carrying their snowboard over her shoulder. Darcy was waiting at a table in the corner.

Stephanie sat down and sighed. "I spent more time snow*sitting* than snowboarding," she said.

Darcy laughed. "It wasn't really that bad, was it?"

"Well, I managed to stay on the board for about ten feet," Stephanie replied. "It's an improvement. And Allie did pretty well."

"Yeah, I did great!" Allie exclaimed. "I mean, I'm no expert, but I am definitely improving."

"How's the ankle, Darce?" Stephanie asked.

Darcy brightened. "Tons better! The ice really did the trick. I think I can definitely ski tomorrow . . . that is, after Maria Cruz checks me out and says it's okay."

"All right!" Stephanie cried. She and Allie each slapped Darcy a high five.

"Snow Jazz is back in business!" Stephanie lifted her glass of water to make a toast. "Here's to victory tomorrow!"

Darcy and Allie clinked water glasses with her. "Long live Snow Jazz!" Allie declared.

"And to one whole wonderful day of humiliation for the Flamingoes," Darcy added.

"But first let's beat the Flamingoes at the scavenger hunt tonight," Stephanie said.

"Right. I'm going to eat a huge dinner," Allie said. "I want to have tons of energy for this."

As soon as dinner was over, Stephanie and her friends hurried to the social hall. Stephanie couldn't wait for the scavenger hunt to begin.

Everyone sat on the floor by teams again. "Hey, Melody got the message," Darcy said. She pointed across the room. Stephanie saw Melody sitting with Dana Michaelson and Kira Shore.

"Good," Stephanie said. "We finally have the team we want. Just the three of us!" Stephanie looked up and groaned. "Almost, anyway," she added.

Michelle was heading her way.

Stephanie sighed. "Oh, well," she said. "I avoided Michelle since lunchtime. But I know how much she wants to be on our scavenger hunt team."

"What should we do?" Darcy asked.

"Nothing," Stephanie said. "We have to let her. What else can we do?"

"You're right," Allie agreed. "Your dad said you have to include Michelle in everything."

"Well, I'll *include* her," Stephanie grumbled. "But that doesn't mean I have to be happy about it."

Mr. Merin waited for the group to settle down. Then he explained the rules of the game.

"Each team has to find all ten items on the list," he told them. "You are not allowed to leave the lodge. You must not take anything without permission from the owner, and above all you can't destroy any property. The first team to bring me all ten items wins the game!" Mr. Merin handed out the lists.

Allie was the first to read the list. "Oh, no! This is tough! Wait until you see this," she cried. "There's some weird stuff on here."

"Well, let's take our time," Stephanie suggested. "Let's stay calm and think about where we could find this stuff before running off on a wild goose chase."

All around the room kids were scattering to start searching.

"Good idea," Allie agreed.

"Let's review everything," Darcy said.

Stephanie read out loud: "A purple mitten, a ski instructor's name badge, an empty hot cocoa packet, a shoe filled with snow, lip balm, ski wax, a shampoo whose brand name contains the letters *s-n-o-w*, something that says Tahoe Lodge on it, a map, a whistle.

"A whistle! Stephanie shrieked. She clapped her hands over her mouth. "Oops, sorry," she whispered, taking her hands away. "But my dad's the only one on this trip who has a whistle. Everyone is going to be after it!"

"But he's *your* father," Darcy pointed out. "He has to give it to you, right?"

"He'd better," Stephanie declared. Then she thought about how annoyed with her he'd seemed after lunch when she'd complained about having Michelle on her team. She hoped that wouldn't hurt her chances of getting his whistle.

Unless . . .

If I send Michelle to get the whistle, Dad will see that I really am including Michelle! He'll give Michelle the whistle for sure!

"Okay," she said. "Here's the plan. We'll each be assigned certain items. Michelle, why don't you get the whistle from Dad? But you have to go right away—everyone is going to try and get that whistle."

"Okay. But what about all the other stuff on the list?" Michelle asked. "Can I help with that, too?"

"Don't worry about it," Stephanie assured her. "Allie, Darcy, and I will split up the rest of the list. Your job is the most important. Just get that whistle. Now go. Hurry!"

Michelle stood reluctantly. "But I wanted to go with you guys," she said. "Maybe we don't need Dad's whistle anyway. We could—"

Stephanie sighed impatiently. "Michelle, you want to help us win, right?"

Michelle nodded.

"Then go. And hurry."

Michelle pressed her lips together tightly, then marched off.

"Okay," Stephanie read on. "The purple mitten and the lip balm—that's easy. Darcy, you have that stuff. And Allie, do you still have that packet of hot cocoa mix in your pocket that you were saving for later?"

Allie nodded eagerly. "Yup. I can just empty it out."

"Good. Now, what shampoo do you guys have? I have Shine On. It only has an *s*, *n*, and *o*."

Darcy thought for a moment. "Mine's just called Apple Shampoo."

Allie's eyes lit up. "Wondrous Shine," she exclaimed. "That's what I use."

Stephanie and Darcy both grinned. "Excellent!" Stephanie cried. "So that's four items. If we get the whistle, that's five. Now, what about ski wax? What is ski wax, anyway?"

"It's wax you put on your skis to keep them in good condition," Darcy explained. "And I think I know where to get some—from the supply closet near the boot rental shed."

Allie stared at her. "How do you know that?"

Darcy made a face. "Because I've been hanging around the lodge all day with nothing to do. I know this place backward by now."

"Okay, we have item number six. Four more." Stephanie closed her eyes to think. "Where can we find a map?"

"At a gas station?" Allie suggested.

Stephanie shook her head. "No, we can't leave

the lodge, remember?" She thought some more. "Hold on. I've got it. On the back of the door in our room—there's a map of the second floor! It shows all the fire exits in case of an emergency. We can use that."

Darcy grinned. "Good thinking, Steph."

Allie patted her on the back. "We're doing great. Only three more items."

Stephanie read the list again. "A ski instructor's name badge, something that says Tahoe Lodge on it, and a shoe filled with snow. How are we going to get a shoe filled with snow if we can't go outside?" she wondered.

"Easy," Allie said. "We open the window in the girls' bathroom and scoop some off the ledge."

Stephanie was impressed. "Good idea. But we'll have to get that one last . . . or the snow will melt."

"A ski instructor's name badge," Darcy said. She shook her head. "That's going to be tough. We don't know any of the ski instructors."

"We'll deal with that later," Stephanie told her. "Let's go collect the stuff we know we have. Come on."

Together they raced upstairs to their room. They put all the items they had into Stephanie's empty duffel bag.

"Hey! Look at this," Stephanie exclaimed. She hurried over to Michelle's bed. "Here's our ninth item—a Tahoe Lodge T-shirt. Michelle bought it for D.J." Stephanie shoved it in the duffel with everything else. "I'm sure she won't mind if we use it."

They ran back downstairs with the duffel bag. The other kids they passed along the way tried to hide the items they had collected. Stephanie couldn't believe how secretive everyone was acting.

"Hurry," Stephanie whispered. She ran down the rest of the stairs to the lobby. Michelle met them by the door to the social hall.

"Did you get it?" Stephanie whispered.

"No," Michelle said. "Dad wasn't in his room."

"Michelle! You should have looked for him," Stephanie snapped. "We need that whistle."

"I'm sorry, Stephanie," Michelle snapped back. "But I thought you could use—"

"Forget it, Michelle," Stephanie exclaimed. "Now, thanks to you, we're going to lose." She turned to Allie and Darcy. "Come on—we have to find my dad."

"Looking for me?" Danny asked. He entered the lobby with two pretty women Stephanie had never seen before.

"Dad! We need your whistle!" she cried.

"My whistle?" Danny asked, looking puzzled. "What's going on tonight, anyway? Everybody keeps asking me for my whistle."

Stephanie's eyes widened. "It's for the scavenger hunt. You didn't give it away, did you?"

Danny laughed. "Nope."

Stephanie sighed. "Great. Then can we have it?"

"Sorry, hon. But I'll tell you what I told everyone else—I lost the whistle this afternoon. Dropped it in the snow." He shook his head. "What a shame. I really loved that whistle."

Stephanie, Allie, and Darcy all groaned.

"Terrific." Stephanie sighed. "Now what? We don't have a whistle or a ski instructor's name badge."

"Uh, excuse me," one of the pretty women said. "I'm Drina. I work here as a ski instructor."

Drina reached into her pocket and pulled out her name badge. "You can borrow this if you'd like."

Stephanie and the others cheered with delight. "Thanks, Drina! You're the best."

"But we still don't have a whistle," Allie pointed out.

Michelle thrust a small piece of wood into Stephanie's hand. She cleared her throat. "I tried to tell you, Stephanie," she began. "I *have* a whistle. Drina showed me how to make one out of bark this afternoon. She told me all good skiers learn how to make them. Then if they get lost, they can whistle for help."

Darcy jumped up and down excitedly. "That's it! We did it!"

"All right!" Allie cried.

Stephanie stared at the whistle. "Michelle, I can't believe you actually made this. That's pretty cool." She raised her hand to give Michelle a high five, but Michelle turned away. She stomped across the lobby.

If that's the way she wants it, fine with me, Stephanie thought.

"I don't blame Michelle for being mad," Danny told her. "After the way you've been treating her."

"What do you mean?" Stephanie protested. "I've been *nice* to her. I let her hang around with us all day and be on our team and stuff. Plus I was even going to let Michelle hand the duffel bag to Mr. Merin."

She turned to Darcy and Allie. "Forget about Michelle," she told them. "Darcy, check the list."

"We only need the last item," Darcy said. "The shoe filled with snow."

Stephanie pulled the shoe from her duffel bag.

"I know where to get it!" Allie exclaimed. She

grabbed the shoe away and raced back up the stairs.

At the same moment the Flamingoes raced downstairs. Rene, Mary, Julie, and Alyssa crossed the lobby. They were laughing and gloating. And holding up an overstuffed bag.

"Oh, no!" Stephanie wailed. "They're heading for Mr. Melin! The Flamingoes won the scavenger hunt!"

CHAPTER
13

◆ ◀ ◗ ◆

Stephanie and Darcy followed the Flamingoes into the social hall. Rene presented their items to Mr. Merin.

Stephanie groaned. "They're going to win. I can't believe this. We were so close."

Mr. Merin checked the items off his list one by one. It looked as though Stephanie was right—the Flamingoes had everything on the list. Even a whistle. Stephanie wondered where they'd managed to find *that.*

Then Mr. Merin held up the last item—and shook his head.

"Sorry, girls," he said. "But the list calls for a shoe filled with *snow.*" He turned it upside down. "Not a shoe filled with *water.* This snow melted."

"The Flamingoes *don't* win!" Stephanie grabbed Darcy and shook her. "We still have a chance!"

Just then Allie ran in. "I got it!" she cried.

Stephanie and Darcy squealed. They raced up to Mr. Merin.

"Here's our *snow*-filled shoe!" Allie exclaimed.

Stephanie handed him the duffel bag. Mr. Merin checked the rest of the items off their list.

"Looks like we have a winner," he declared. "Snow Jazz!"

Stephanie, Allie, and Darcy cheered.

"And to prove that victory is sweet, here's your prize." Mr. Merin handed them an extra-giant-size box of chocolate chip cookies.

"Thanks, Mr. Merin!" Stephanie exclaimed. She nudged Allie and Darcy. "You know what the best part of this is?" she whispered. "The *sour* expression on Rene's face!"

They all burst out laughing. It was a great moment.

"Wait a minute. Aren't you missing a team-mate?" Mr. Merin suddenly asked. "Where is Melody Kimball?"

"Oh, she's around somewhere," Stephanie told him.

"Well, you'd better go find her and tell her that

you won," Mr. Merin said. "She might still be hunting for items!"

"Right! We'll look in our room," Stephanie promised. She, Allie, and Darcy hurried back to their bedroom. Michelle followed them. Stephanie handed around the cookie box, and they all munched happily.

Except for Michelle. She refused to eat. She sat on her bed without saying a word.

Fine, Stephanie thought. *Let her sulk. I tried to be nice.*

"Did you see the look on Rene's face?" Allie asked again.

"That's nothing compared to how she's going to look tomorrow—when we ace that relay race," Stephanie replied.

"Oooh. I just had the most amazing idea." Darcy swallowed the last bit of cookie in her mouth. "Let's raid Rene's room!"

Stephanie's eyes lit up. "What an excellent idea! We can sneak in and cover the place with toilet paper. That will get back at her for being such a cheat at the sing-down."

Allie giggled. "We could do it while everyone's down at the big party later."

Michelle sat up eagerly. "Can I come, too?" she asked.

Allie glanced at Stephanie. "Why not let her come, Steph?" she asked. "After all, she did help us win the scavenger hunt."

Stephanie shook her head. "No, I don't think it would be such a good idea. Dad would kill me if he found out I let Michelle break the rules."

"But he won't find out," Michelle protested.

"No, Michelle. It isn't a good idea. If we get caught, we could get in a lot of trouble. I'll tell you what, though. To thank you for helping us win the scavenger hunt, you can hang with us all day tomorrow. How's that?" Stephanie asked.

Michelle frowned. "Big whoop," she muttered.

Stephanie shrugged. "Suit yourself." She turned back to Darcy and Allie. "Okay, and how about smearing lip gloss on the inside doorknob? It'll be a blast!"

Suddenly there was a commotion outside their room.

Stephanie jumped up and flung open the door.

"Melody! What are *you* doing here?" Stephanie demanded.

"I . . . I, uh, came to get the rest of my stuff," Melody said.

"Oh, sure," Stephanie replied. "Like you weren't just eavesdropping on our conversation."

Melody shook her head. "I wasn't. I just came to get my sleeping bag and pillow."

Melody grabbed the sleeping bag and pillow from what had been her bed.

Stephanie felt a teeny twinge of guilt. What if Allie was right? What if Melody *had* been telling the truth?

Couldn't be, she told herself.

"Well, I'll be going now," Melody said. "I'm going to bunk with Kira Shore and Dana Michaelson. But I'll still snowboard on your team tomorrow if you want," she added.

Stephanie glanced at Darcy and Allie. Melody really did seem genuinely sad. Still . . .

"Sorry. But we don't really need another snowboarder," Stephanie said at last. "Michelle is on our team. And we have Darcy back, too. So we still have four members."

Melody managed a small smile. "Well, I'm glad your ankle is better, Darcy," she said.

"Uh, thanks, Melody," Darcy muttered.

"Oh, and congratulations on wining the scavenger hunt," Melody added. She left the room.

Stephanie collapsed onto her bed. "We're doing the right thing, aren't we?" she asked her friends. "I mean, the Flamingoes are *always* double-crossing

111

us *somehow*. This thing with Melody—it *has* to be part of a big plan to get us or something. Right?"

Allie shrugged. "I guess so," Darcy said.

Stephanie sighed. "Then why do I feel so crummy about it?"

The party was in full swing. But Stephanie, Allie, and Darcy slipped out of the social hall. It was time for the big raid. They raced upstairs to their room. Stephanie had swiped three rolls of toilet paper from the girls' bathroom. Darcy found her lip gloss. Allie had made a sign that said SNOW JAZZ RULES. They crept down the hall toward Rene's room, trying not to giggle.

This is going to be great," Stephanie whispered.

Darcy snickered. "I wish I could see their faces when they come upstairs and find this!"

Stephanie chuckled. "Me too."

"Stephanie. You have to stop laughing. Someone will hear us," Darcy scolded.

Stephanie covered her mouth with her hand. "Sorry," she mumbled. "I'm okay now. Let's go."

They reached Rene's room. Quietly Stephanie reached out and turned the doorknob. The door swung open. Stephanie, Allie, and Darcy slipped inside.

The room was very dark. Stephanie blinked a

few times, trying to adjust to the darkness. Then the lights suddenly flashed on. And something wet poured all over her body.

"Wha—?" Stephanie cried. She was completely drenched.

"Hey! We're soaking wet!" Darcy exclaimed.

"That'll teach you to try and outsmart the Flamingoes," Rene sang out.

Julie, Mary, and Alyssa snickered and held up their empty water buckets.

Rene pointed a camera. "Say 'losers,' " she cried, snapping a picture.

Stephanie was too stunned to speak. Her clothes were soaked through. Her hair was matted down to her head. And she was holding three rolls of totally soggy toilet paper.

"That picture will look great on the first page of the *Scribe*," Rene shouted. "What do you think, Flamingoes?"

"Can I get a copy for my locker?" Mary joked.

Stephanie grabbed Allie's wrist. She pushed Darcy ahead of her. "Let's get out of here," she said.

Back in their room Michelle gasped when she saw them. "Wow you're a mess. Uh—who did that?" she asked.

Stephanie grabbed her towel and began to dry

herself off. "Rene! She was waiting for us with buckets of water."

"Rene threw water on you?" Michelle asked.

"What does it look like?" Stephanie said angrily.

"Look at me!" Allie cried. She twisted her shirt. A stream of water ran out and made a puddle on the floor. Darcy wrapped her own head in a towel to dry.

"But how did she know you were coming?" Michelle asked.

"How do you think they knew?" Stephanie asked. "It was Melody again. She was listening at the door and heard everything. And to think I almost gave her a second chance."

"Once a Flamingo, always a Flamingo," Darcy muttered.

Stephanie changed into dry clothes. "You know what this means," she said to her friends. "This means revenge on all the Flamingoes. And an extra-special revenge for their spy—Melody Kimball!"

CHAPTER
14

◆ ◀ ◆ ◆

Brriiing!

Stephanie opened her eyes and groaned. "Ugh! It's too early to get up!"

Darcy moaned and rolled over in her sleeping bag. "Is it eight o'clock?" she asked.

"No," Allie replied. "Six. We're getting up early for that snowboarding lesson, remember?"

"Can't we sleep a little longer?" Darcy asked.

"No," Stephanie said. "This is the big day!" She swung her legs over the side of the bed and stretched. "Today is the relay race, remember? We *need* that lesson! We have to beat the Flamingoes today—especially after last night!"

Allie pulled herself up. "Steph is right, Darcy.

We have to get there early or we'll miss the lesson. You too, Michelle. Wake up!"

Michelle groaned from her bed. "Okay, okay. I'm up!"

They quickly dressed and made their way downstairs. The lobby was deserted. Stephanie led the way to the desk where they had been told to sign up for private lessons.

"We're here for a private snowboarding lesson," she told the man behind the counter.

The man frowned. "Oh, I'm sorry," he said. "But Drina and Dirk are already out giving lessons." He pointed outside.

Stephanie turned—and saw Drina walking with Rene! They each had a snowboard tucked under one arm. Drina and Rene were followed by Julie, Alyssa, and Mary.

"No way!" Stephanie wailed. "I can't believe it! They beat us out again!"

Rene waved as she walked past. "Too bad!" she shouted at them. "Guess you should have woken up earlier!"

Stephanie turned to Darcy. "Darcy, it's up to you. You have to teach us *everything* you know about snowboarding! We have to beat the Flamingoes today. Or . . . or I don't know *what* I'll do!"

Darcy nodded. "No problem, Steph. Let's get

some boards and hit the powder. I'll have you three gliding at top speed in no time!"

Darcy showed them how to glide, how to turn, how to shift weight, and how to stop. The only thing she couldn't do was actually ride the snowboard herself. She still had to wait for Maria Cruz to check out her ankle.

By breakfast time Stephanie, Allie, and Michelle had all improved. Stephanie was even able to turn left with total control. Now that she had the hang of it, snowboarding was actually fun!

Allie slapped Stephanie a high five as they walked back to the lodge. "You're doing so much better," she said. "You know, I think we might even have a chance at beating the Flamingoes."

"Of course we do!" Stephanie scoffed. "Our team is a zillion times better than theirs! Don't you think so, Michelle?"

Michelle shrugged. "I guess."

"What's with you, Michelle?" Stephanie asked. "You've been quiet all morning."

"Nothing," Michelle mumbled.

"Look, I said I was sorry for getting on your case about the whistle, okay?" Stephanie asked.

Michelle didn't answer.

She still wants to pout, Stephanie thought. *Then fine! Let her pout! I'm not going to let her ruin my day.*

"Anyway, we should all meet here for more practice after Darcy gets her ankle checked," Stephanie went on. "The race is at one, and we don't want to waste any valuable practice time."

They brought back their snowboards. Then they headed into the cafeteria and found a table for breakfast. Lara Hayes and Ellen Shapiro, two girls from the Sassy Skiers, passed their table.

"How was your shower last night, Stephanie?" Ellen asked. She and Lara giggled and hurried away, whispering.

Stephanie's face turned red. "Rene must have told everyone about last night!" She groaned. "Now they're all laughing at us!"

Kyle and his friends from the Downhill Dudes stopped at the table next. One of them tossed a bar of soap at Stephanie. Even Kyle laughed. The rest of his friends ran away, hooting with laughter.

"Oh, man, this is so embarrassing!" Darcy exclaimed.

A waiter appeared carrying a tray filled with water glasses. "Those girls over there said you needed water at this table." He pointed across the room. Stephanie glanced up. Rene, Mary, Julie, and Alyssa waved at her, grinning.

Everyone in their section of the cafeteria burst out laughing.

"This is more than embarrassing," Allie murmured. "This is *humiliating*."

The commotion finally died down. Stephanie leaned over the table. "Okay, people," she whispered. "I just thought of the perfect revenge! I call it Operation Iced Birds."

Stephanie stopped to make sure Melody was nowhere around. She spotted her sitting with Kira and Dana a few tables away.

Allie laughed. "Sounds good. But whisper because those Flamingoes keep walking by."

Stephanie nodded. The Flamingoes had to go right past their table to get refills of juice and hot cocoa.

"Remember, Melody said Rene was hiding the pink jackets in the closet," she whispered. "They're only going to wear them in the big race."

Allie and Darcy nodded.

"So we sneak into their room when they're *not* wearing them and hide them! They'll flip when they don't have their lucky jackets for the big race."

Darcy's eyes brightened. "I like it!" she said. "When are we going to do this?"

"Right after lunch, while the Flamingoes are still eating," Stephanie replied. "Allie, you'll stay down here and keep watch while Darcy and I go upstairs to steal the jackets. If they finish eating too soon, you can race up the back staircase and warn us."

"What do I do?" Michelle whispered.

Stephanie shook her head. "Nothing. This doesn't concern you, Michelle. You weren't part of the raid last night."

"But I want to help!" Michelle insisted. "Come on, Stephanie! You never let me do anything!"

"That's not true, Michelle," Stephanie retorted. "I'm letting you race with us today, remember? Come on, don't be such a baby."

Michelle's face reddened. "I'm not being a baby," she said.

"Just forget about it, Michelle. It doesn't involve you. You don't even go to school with the Flamingoes. Darcy, should we come with you to see Maria Cruz?"

Darcy nodded, and Stephanie and Allie followed her to Maria's table. They all held their breath as Maria examined Darcy's ankle.

"It does look much better," Maria agreed. "I guess it will be okay for you to ski today. But please, be careful! And give your ankle a rest every now and then."

Darcy clasped her hands together. "Excellent! Thank you so much!"

Stephanie and Allie cheered. "Now come on, let's hit the slopes!" Darcy cried.

Allie looked around. "Where's Michelle?" she asked.

Stephanie didn't see her sister anywhere. "Probably sulking again. Or whining to my father. Don't worry about her. We have to concentrate on snowboarding."

Stephanie put her arms around her two best friends. "Just keep picturing this," she added happily. "The Flamingoes . . . as our personal slaves. For a whole day!"

CHAPTER
15

◆ ◀ ◆ ◆

"Okay, guys," Darcy instructed, "to make a turn, you have to bend your knees and balance your whole body over them." She hopped onto a snowboard to demonstrate.

Stephanie and Allie watched in amazement as Darcy soared down the slope, turning left, then right every few feet.

"Wow!" Stephanie gushed. "You're awesome!"

Darcy grinned. "Now you guys give it a try."

For the entire morning Stephanie and Allie hung on Darcy's every word and followed her every move. By lunchtime Darcy had turned Stephanie and Allie into pretty decent snowboarders.

At lunch the girls gobbled up their sandwiches. Then it was time for Operation Iced Birds.

"Where are you going to put the pink parkas after you steal them?" Allie asked.

Stephanie wore a mischievous grin. "I was thinking we'd stuff them all into Melody's sleeping bag!"

Darcy and Allie both smiled. "You're a genius!" Allie cried. "That's a great idea."

"But we need to make sure that Melody isn't in her room when we do it. Maybe we can send Michelle to find out," Stephanie said.

"Where is Michelle, anyway?" Darcy asked.

"Oh, she's eating lunch with my dad," Stephanie said, glancing about the room. "We'd better forget about using Michelle. But we should get upstairs. The Flamingoes are almost done with their lunches."

Stephanie and Darcy casually left the table and headed for the door. Allie remained in the dining room to keep an eye on the Flamingoes.

Stephanie and Darcy dashed up the stairs toward the Flamingoes' room. They opened the door and slipped inside. Stephanie ran to the closet and flung open the door. The closet was empty.

"The parkas aren't here!" Darcy said.

"That's weird," Stephanie remarked. "They weren't wearing them outside this morning. Or at lunch. But we saw them wearing the jackets on the bus."

They searched the room, but the pink parkas were nowhere in sight.

"Maybe Melody heard us discussing the plan. Did she tip off Rene and the others?"

Darcy shook her head. "No way. I checked to see where Melody was whenever we talked about the plan. She couldn't have overheard."

Stephanie took a deep breath. "Let's get out of here," she said. "It's almost time for the race."

Back in the dining room Allie glanced up eagerly. "How did it go?" she whispered.

"It didn't go," Stephanie replied. "The jackets weren't there!"

"Are you sure? Did you check everywhere?" Allie asked.

Stephanie nodded. "We can't figure it out," she said. "The Flamingoes aren't wearing the jackets."

"Weird," Allie muttered. "But maybe one of the other Flamingoes overheard our plan. Julie Chu kept walking past our table this morning, remember?"

Stephanie nodded. "True. Any of them might have heard."

Mr. Merin stood up. "The snowboarding relay race will begin in exactly one-half hour," he said.

"Everyone will meet at the course and stand next to the sign with their team name."

Stephanie sighed. The mystery of the missing pink parkas was going to remain a mystery.

"Forget about the parkas," she said. "The race is more important anyway. Are you guys ready?"

Darcy and Allie both smiled. "Ready!"

"Good! Let's get Michelle and head over to the course." She hurried to her father's table.

"Please wear your knee pads, Stephanie," her father said in a concerned voice.

"Okay, Dad!" Stephanie said. "Stop worrying! We're all going to be fine! Now, where did Michelle go?"

"To meet the team at the course," Danny replied. "And I'll see you out there, too. I'm blowing the starting whistle! I'll use Michelle's bark whistle. I'm the official referee!"

"Good for you, Dad." Stephanie grinned. Her father had finally found a good use for his whistle.

Outside, everyone gathered for the start of the race. Stephanie, Allie, and Darcy stood by the sign that said Snow Jazz.

"This is it, you guys!" Stephanie said. "We're going to beat the ski pants off the Flamingoes!"

"Yeah. But where is Michelle?" Darcy asked.

Stephanie scanned the crowd. "I couldn't get rid

of her all weekend," she complained. "But now, when we need her, we can't find her anywhere!"

Mr. Merin gave their final instructions. "Here's how the race works," he called out. "The first person on your team comes down to the red flag and pulls it off the post. Then the next person snowboards to the blue flag . . ."

Stephanie stopped listening. She searched again for Michelle. Where was she, anyway? She was going to miss the whole race!

"Oh, no!" Allie exclaimed.

Stephanie spun around. "Allie, what is it?" she asked.

Allie pointed across the slope. Stephanie and Darcy followed her gaze. The Flamingoes stood next to their Iced Flamingoes sign. And they were wearing their pink parkas!

Darcy's jaw dropped open. "How did they get their jackets without us seeing them?" she asked.

"Yeah, and how—" Stephanie gasped. "Michelle!"

Michelle was standing with Rene and the Flamingoes. And she was wearing one of Rene's thick pink sweaters!

"What's she doing with them?" Darcy demanded.

"I don't know," Stephanie said, "but I'm going

to find out!" She stomped over to the Flamingoes sign. "Michelle, just what is going on?"

"I'm on this team now," Michelle replied.

Rene shot Stephanie a smug smile. "Didn't you know, Stephanie? Michelle is our star snowboarder."

Stephanie's jaw dropped. "Michelle, are you crazy? How could you join the Iced Flamingoes?"

"Because *they've* been nice to me!" Michelle replied. "They *want* me on their team!"

Stephanie pulled her sister aside. "You can't do this, Michelle. They're the enemy!" she exclaimed.

"Not *my* enemy," Michelle said. "They let me hang around with them and ask any questions I want."

"So you've been hanging around with Rene all weekend?" Stephanie asked.

Michelle nodded. "And I tell them anything they want to know."

"Anything?" Stephanie asked.

"Whatever they need to know," Michelle said.

Stephanie had a terrible sinking feeling in her stomach. Suddenly everything began to make sense.

She was so sure that Melody told the Flamingoes everything. But she wasn't at all sure now. She thought over all the tricks the Flamingoes had played:

The Snow Spaz sign on Stephanie's back. Telling everyone about "Rufus." Knowing the song "In a Yellow Mood." Knowing about the failed toilet paper raid. And . . . *Operation Iced Birds!*

Michelle had known about all those things.

The spy wasn't Melody after all. It was Michelle!

"Okay," Mr. Merin's voice boomed through the bullhorn. "One last practice run, then let the race begin!"

Stephanie ignored him. "Michelle, tell me it wasn't you. You couldn't have told Rene everything!"

"It *was* me, okay?" Michelle folded her arms stubbornly over her chest.

Stephanie stared at her little sister in disbelief. "But you know I can't stand the Flamingoes! How could you do that?"

"Because I was sick of how you were treating me!" Michelle blurted. "It wasn't fair! You made me promise to be quiet this weekend, and I was! You made me promise not to ask a million questions, and I didn't! But you still kept leaving me out of everything!"

"I did not—" Stephanie began to protest. She

stopped and thought about everything Michelle said.

"You know, I was just so mad at the Flamingoes," Stephanie finally said. "I didn't notice how much I was hurting your feelings, Michelle. I guess I have been pretty awful. You're right."

"I'm *right?*" Michelle asked.

Stephanie nodded. "Yes. It's my fault. I drove you to your life as a spy. I didn't give you any choice. I should have been nicer."

Michelle frowned. "Yeah! You should have been!"

"I feel really bad about it, Michelle," Stephanie said. "Rene and the Flamingoes bring out the worst in me. But I'm sorry I took it all out on you. Can I make it up to you?"

"How?" Michelle asked.

"Well, from now on you can be an *official* member of the Snow Jazz team," Stephanie replied. "To be included in every activity. And to share in every victory. Including this race! If we win it, that is. Do you accept?"

"Definitely!" Michelle cried. She whispered in Stephanie's ear, "These Flamingo girls are pretty nasty, anyway. I didn't like them one bit!"

Stephanie laughed.

Michelle slipped off the pink sweater. She tossed

it to Rene. "This sweater is too ugly for me," she said. "I changed my mind. I'd rather race for Snow Jazz." She and Stephanie hurried back to Darcy and Allie.

"Here, Michelle. You'd better wear this." Stephanie pulled off her orange parka and handed it to Michelle. Michelle put it on and rolled up the sleeves.

"But what will you wear?" Michelle asked.

"I'll try to find another jacket," Stephanie answered.

"But Stephanie!" Darcy wailed. "The race is about to start!"

"What else can I do?" she asked. Stephanie turned to go—and bumped smack into someone.

"Melody! Oh, sorry!" Stephanie said. She felt her cheeks turn red.

"That's okay," Melody replied. "I heard what happened with Rene. Seems like you need to borrow a jacket."

Melody was wearing a weird white jacket that Stephanie had never seen before. She carried her purple-and-blue parka. She held it out to Stephanie. "Take this," she said.

Stephanie stared at Melody in surprise. She'd accused Melody of cheating, lying, and spying. But Melody was still being nice to her!

Stephanie slipped the jacket on. "Um, thanks!" she said.

"I know this jacket looks funny," Melody remarked. "It's the pink one. I turned it inside out—since I'm not a Flamingo anymore."

Stephanie swallowed hard. "I'm really sorry, Melody. About everything. I believe you now. I should have believed you all along."

Melody laughed. "It's okay," she said. "I know it's hard to trust the Flamingoes. I only felt bad because I thought you guys were really cool. I thought we could be friends."

Stephanie grinned. "We can be!" she said. "We'd like that a lot, right, guys?"

Allie and Darcy both nodded eagerly.

"Do you feel like coming back on the team?" Stephanie asked.

"Really?" Melody asked.

"Really," Allie said.

"Really," Darcy echoed.

"Then yes!" Melody declared. "Let's bury those pink finks!"

Mr. Merin picked up a huge red bullhorn. "Everybody line up and wait for the starting whistle!" he called.

Stephanie held out her hand. Darcy put her hand on top of Stephanie's, and Allie put hers on top of

Darcy's. Then Michelle and Melody put their hands on top.

"Three cheers for Snow Jazz!" Stephanie cried. "The greatest snowboarding team in the world!"

Mr. Merin held the bullhorn in front of Danny Tanner's mouth. Danny took the bark whistle from his pocket.

"On your mark!" he shouted. "Get set!"

Tweeeeet!

CHAPTER
16

◆ ◀ ◢ ◆

"Go, Melody, go!"

Stephanie shouted loudly as Melody whizzed down the slope on the snowboard. Melody was a great snowboarder!

Melody didn't fall once. She reached the middle of the relay course and pulled a red flag off the post. She handed the flag to Stephanie. Stephanie took a deep breath. If she made it down the rest of the course without too many mistakes, Snow Jazz might win! Stephanie pushed off.

"Come on, Steph!" Darcy shouted from the bottom of the slope. "You can do it!"

Stephanie managed to glide for about ten feet before tumbling off the board.

"Get back up, Stephanie!" Melody cried.

"Shift your weight!" Michelle called out.

"Remember to balance!" Darcy shouted.

Stephanie climbed back onto the board. She pushed off again and shifted her weight. Staring straight ahead, she focused on Melody, who had raced down the course to the finish line.

Melody jumped up and down, waving her hands high above her head. "Aim it here, Stephanie," she called.

Stephanie's board soared straight down the slope. Seconds later she crossed the finish line!

Tweeeet!

Her father's whistle rang out loud and clear. It was the first time that the sound didn't bother her at all.

She made it! Snow Jazz won the race!

Allie, Darcy, Melody, and Michelle raced up to Stephanie. They hugged her and cheered.

"You did it! You did it!" Darcy cried.

"We *all* did it!" Stephanie cheered. "Melody, you didn't tell us you were such a good snowboarder!" she added.

Melody chuckled. "Why do you think Rene was trying so hard to keep me on her team?"

"Speaking of Rene," Allie said, "check out the pink spaz trying to snowboard!"

Everyone stared up the mountain. Rene was teetering awkwardly on her snowboard. She lasted about one second—then fell on her face.

"She looks ridiculous now," Stephanie said with a twinkle in her eye. "But that's nothing— wait till you see how she looks tomorrow at school!"

Stephanie leaned back with her hands behind her head.

Ah, this is the life! she thought. She smiled at Allie, who was sitting just as comfortably. Darcy and Melody stretched in their own chairs.

"How's your pizza, Melody?" Stephanie asked.

Melody shrugged. "I don't know. I haven't tasted it yet."

Stephanie sat up in dismay. "What's taking so long?" She cleared her throat. "Hey, how's the pizza coming, Salter?"

Rene groaned, then mumbled something under her breath.

"What was that, oh personal slave of mine?" Stephanie asked loudly. She hoped everyone in the school cafeteria could hear. "Did you say something?"

Rene sighed. "I *said*," she repeated, "it's almost ready." She continued cutting a slice of pizza into tiny bite-size pieces. She was using a little plastic fork and knife. The knife snapped in half.

"It's hard to move in this stupid orange jacket, you know!" Rene groaned.

Stephanie and her friends laughed. "Well, hurry it up!" Stephanie ordered. "We're hungry!"

"And when you finish cutting pizza for all of us, don't forget about dessert," Darcy told Mary.

"We'll have brownies, cookies, and the fresh fruit cups," Allie added to Julie.

"Right! So hop to it," Stephanie told Alyssa.

She leaned back in her chair again. Just then she spotted her friend Gia, the photographer from the *Scribe*, in the cafeteria.

"Over here, Gia!" she called out.

Gia hurried to their table with her camera.

"Ready to shoot the *Scribe*'s front-page shot for next month?" Stephanie asked.

"Ready!" Gia snapped a picture of Rene and the Flamingoes preparing lunch for Stephanie, Allie, Darcy, and Melody.

"Don't forget to say 'losers!' " Stephanie sang out.

Everyone in the lunchroom—except for the Flamingoes—laughed out loud.

Melody gave Stephanie a high five. "Nice going," she said.

"Hey, Melody," Stephanie called. "Answer this riddle. When *can* you trust a Flamingo?"

Melody seemed confused. "I don't know. When?" she asked.

Stephanie grinned at her new friend. "When she's an *ex*-Flamingo!"

It doesn't matter if you live around the corner...
or around the world...
If you are a fan of Mary-Kate and Ashley Olsen,
you should be a member of

MARY-KATE + ASHLEY'S FUN CLUB™

Here's what you get:
Our Funzine™
An autographed color photo
Two black & white individual photos
A full size color poster
An official **Fun Club**™ membership card
A **Fun Club**™ school folder
Two special **Fun Club**™ surprises
A holiday card
Fun Club™ collectibles catalog
Plus a **Fun Club**™ box to keep everything in

To join Mary-Kate + Ashley's Fun Club™, fill out the form
below and send it along with

U.S. Residents – $17.00
Canadian Residents – $22 U.S. Funds
International Residents – $27 U.S. Funds

MARY-KATE + ASHLEY'S FUN CLUB™
859 HOLLYWOOD WAY, SUITE 275
BURBANK, CA 91505

NAME:_____

ADDRESS:_____

_CITY:_____ STATE:_____ ZIP:_____

PHONE:(____) _____ BIRTHDATE:_____

1242